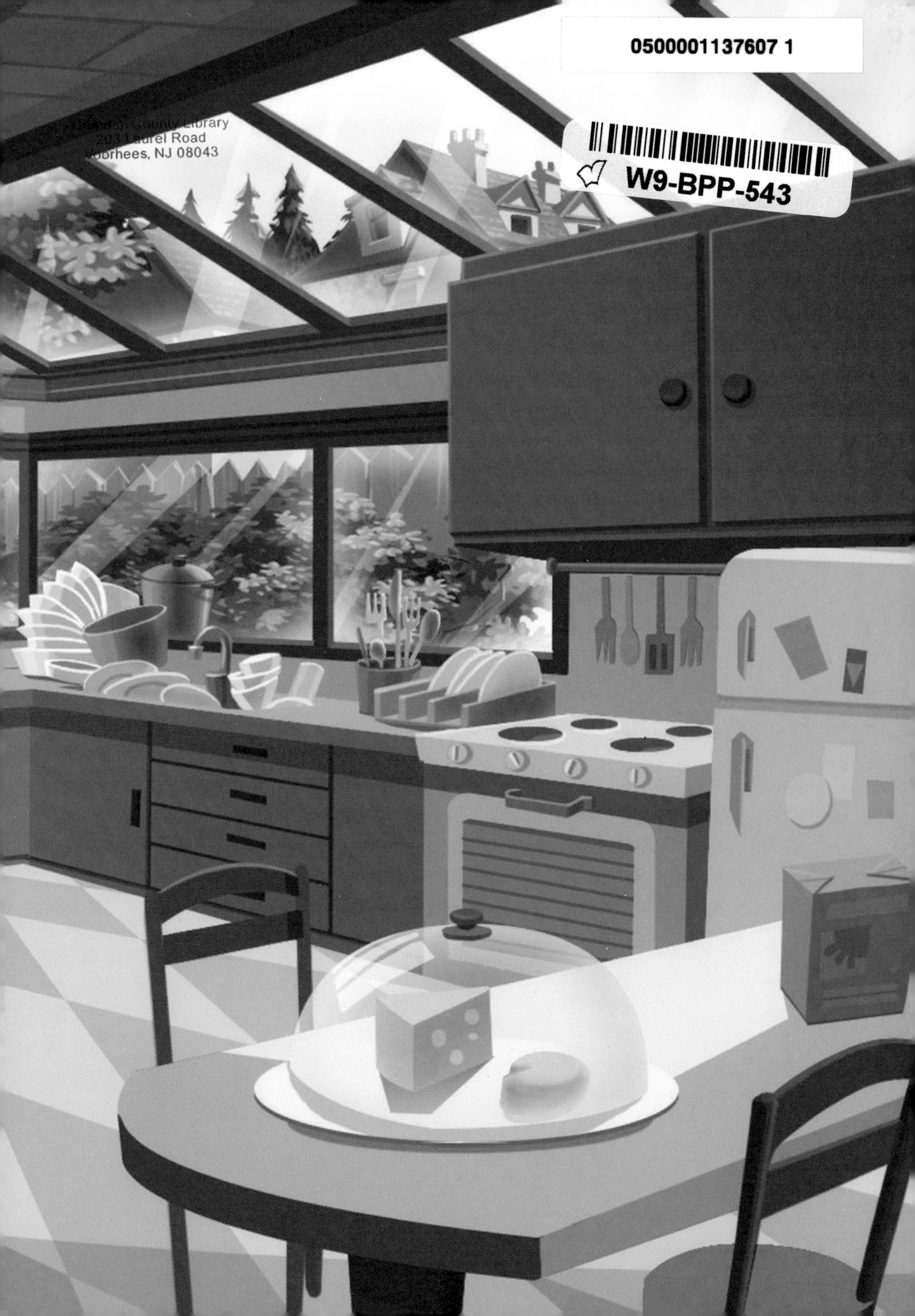

Geronimo Stilton™ Reporter

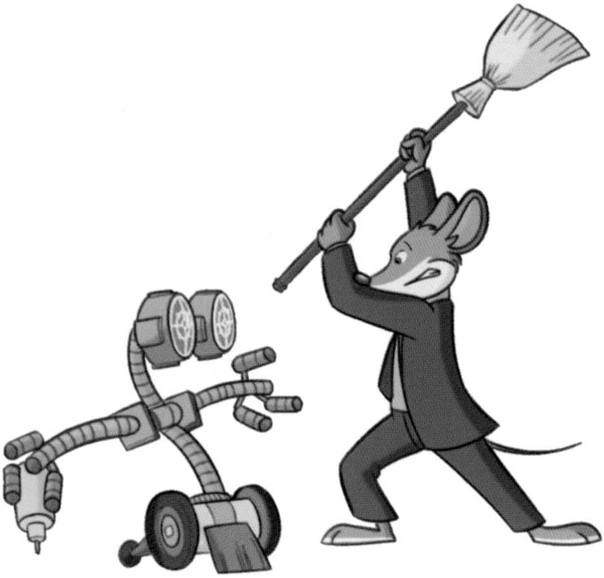

PAPERCUTZ™

Geronimo Stilton

GRAPHIC NOVELS AVAILABLE FROM PAPERCUTZ

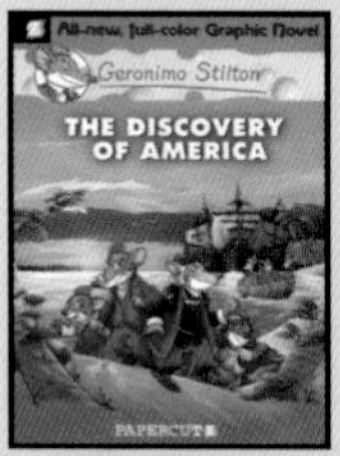
All-new, full-color Graphic Novel
Geronimo Stilton
THE DISCOVERY OF AMERICA
PAPERCUTZ

#1
"The Discovery of America"

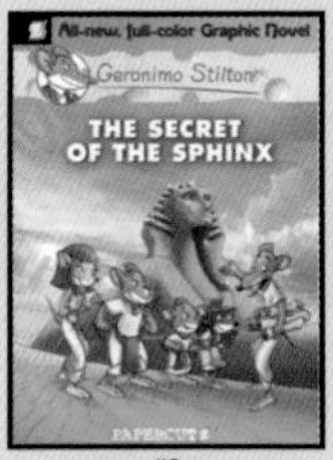
All-new, full-color Graphic Novel
Geronimo Stilton
THE SECRET OF THE SPHINX
PAPERCUTZ

#2
"The Secret of the Sphinx"

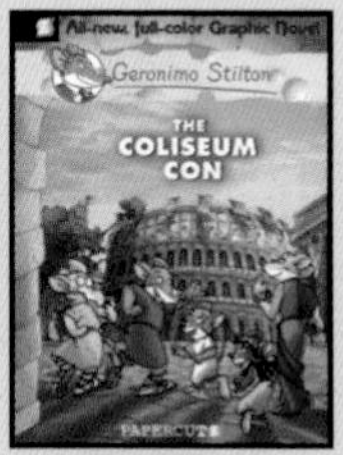
All-new, full-color Graphic Novel
Geronimo Stilton
THE COLISEUM CON
PAPERCUTZ

#3
"The Coliseum Con"

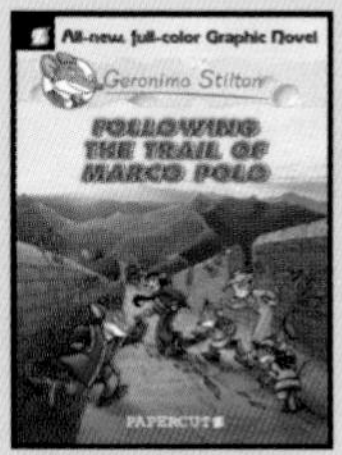
All-new, full-color Graphic Novel
Geronimo Stilton
FOLLOWING THE TRAIL OF MARCO POLO
PAPERCUTZ

#4
"Following the Trail of Marco Polo"

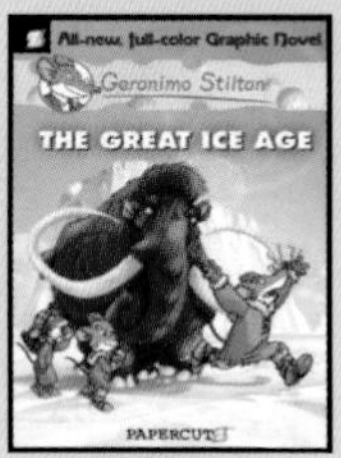
All-new, full-color Graphic Novel
Geronimo Stilton
THE GREAT ICE AGE
PAPERCUTZ

#5
"The Great Ice Age"

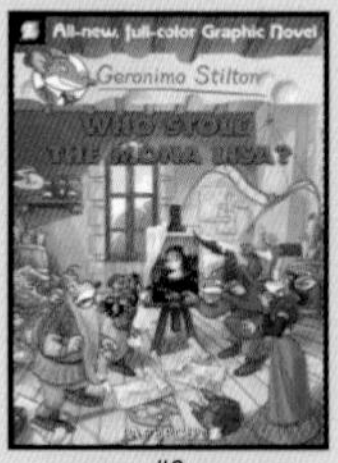
All-new, full-color Graphic Novel
Geronimo Stilton
WHO STOLE THE MONA LISA?

#6
"Who Stole The Mona Lisa?"

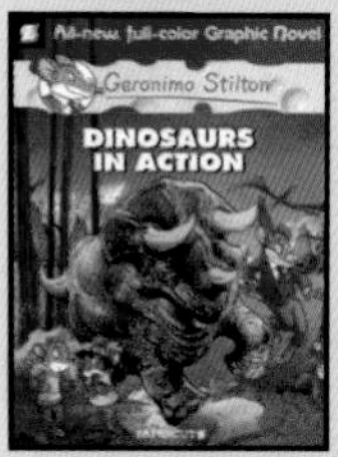
All-new, full-color Graphic Novel
Geronimo Stilton
DINOSAURS IN ACTION
PAPERCUTZ

#7
"Dinosaurs in Action"

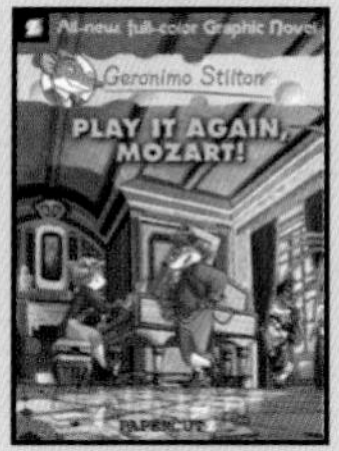
All-new, full-color Graphic Novel
Geronimo Stilton
PLAY IT AGAIN, MOZART!
PAPERCUTZ

#8
"Play It Again, Mozart!"

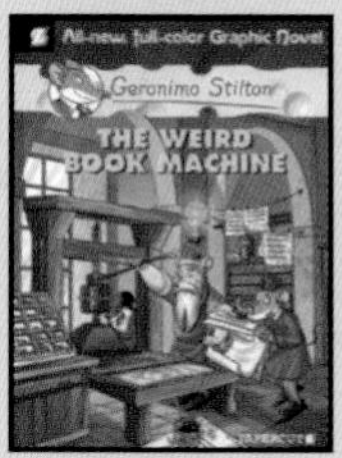
All-new, full-color Graphic Novel
Geronimo Stilton
THE WEIRD BOOK MACHINE
PAPERCUTZ

#9
"The Weird Book Machine"

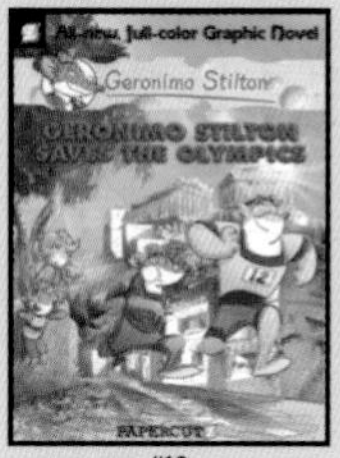
All-new, full-color Graphic Novel
Geronimo Stilton
GERONIMO STILTON SAVES THE OLYMPICS
PAPERCUTZ

#10
"Geronimo Stilton Saves the Olympics"

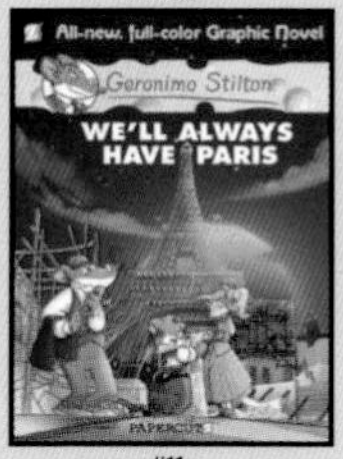
All-new, full-color Graphic Novel
Geronimo Stilton
WE'LL ALWAYS HAVE PARIS
PAPERCUTZ

#11
"We'll Always Have Paris"

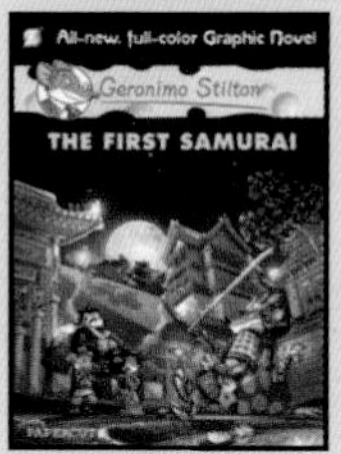
All-new, full-color Graphic Novel
Geronimo Stilton
THE FIRST SAMURAI
PAPERCUTZ

#12
"The First Samurai"

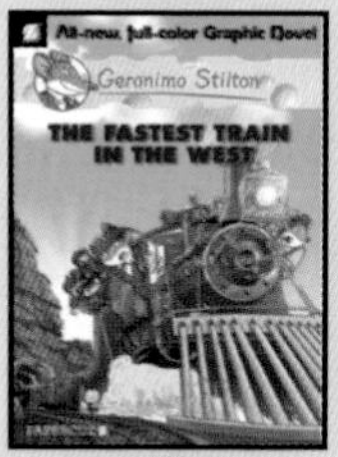
All-new, full-color Graphic Novel
Geronimo Stilton
THE FASTEST TRAIN IN THE WEST
PAPERCUTZ

#13
"The Fastest Train in the West"

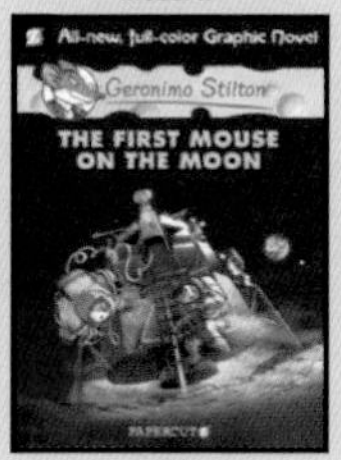
All-new, full-color Graphic Novel
Geronimo Stilton
THE FIRST MOUSE ON THE MOON
PAPERCUTZ

#14
"The First Mouse on the Moon"

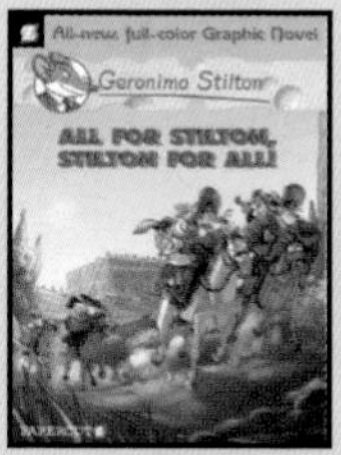
All-new, full-color Graphic Novel
Geronimo Stilton
ALL FOR STILTON, STILTON FOR ALL!
PAPERCUTZ

#15
"All for Stilton, Stilton for All!"

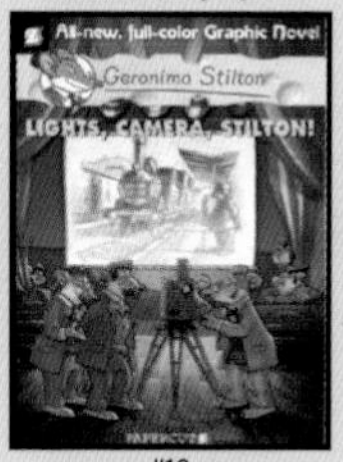
All-new, full-color Graphic Novel
Geronimo Stilton
LIGHTS, CAMERA, STILTON!
PAPERCUTZ

#16
"Lights, Camera, Stilton!"

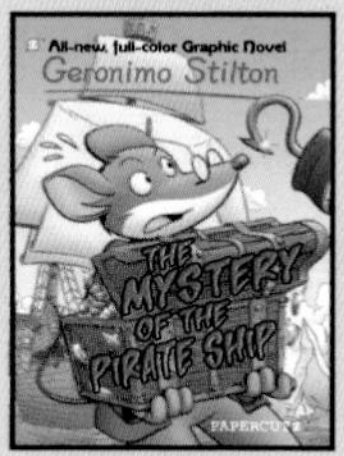
All-new, full-color Graphic Novel
Geronimo Stilton
THE MYSTERY OF THE PIRATE SHIP
PAPERCUTZ

#17
"The Mystery of the Pirate Ship"

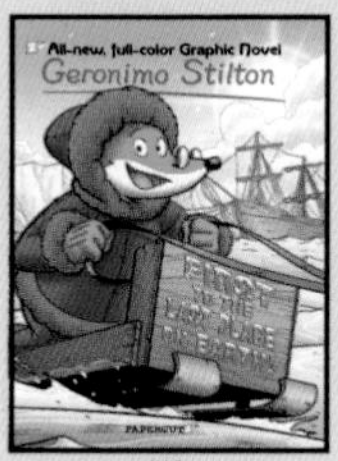
All-new, full-color Graphic Novel
Geronimo Stilton
PAPERCUTZ

#18
"First to the Last Place on Earth"

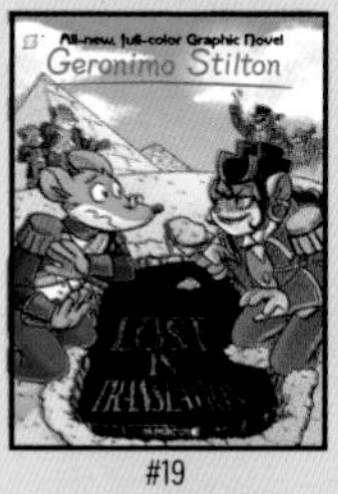
All-new, full-color Graphic Novel
Geronimo Stilton
LOST IN TRANSLATION

#19
"Lost in Translation"

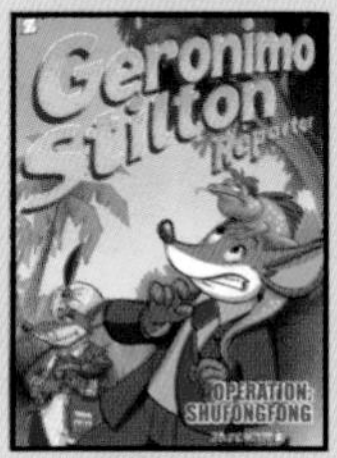
Geronimo Stilton
Reporter
OPERATION: SHUFONGFONG

GERONIMO STILTON REPORTER #1
"Operation ShuFongfong"

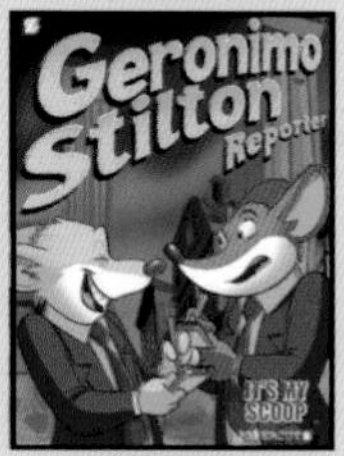
Geronimo Stilton
Reporter
IT'S MY SCOOP

GERONIMO STILTON REPORTER #2
"It's My Scoop"

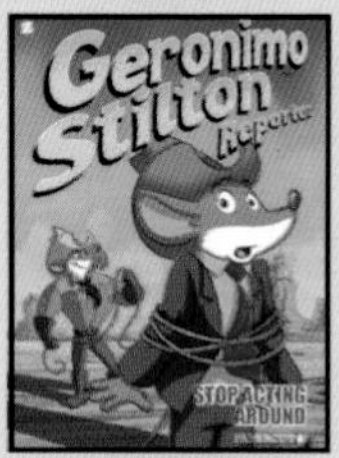
Geronimo Stilton
Reporter
STOP ACTING AROUND

GERONIMO STILTON REPORTER #3
"Stop Acting Around"

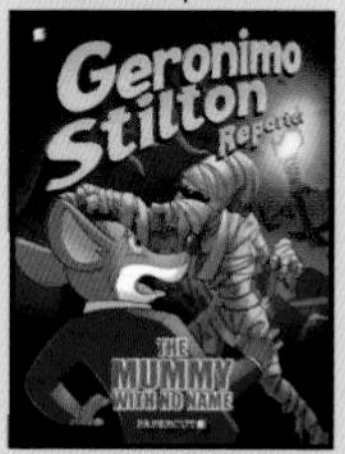
Geronimo Stilton
Reporter
THE MUMMY WITH NO NAME

GERONIMO STILTON REPORTER #4
"The Mummy with No Name"

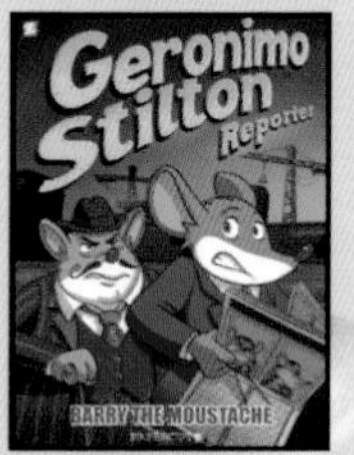
Geronimo Stilton
Reporter
BARRY THE MOUSTACHE

GERONIMO STILTON REPORTER #5
"Barry the Moustache"

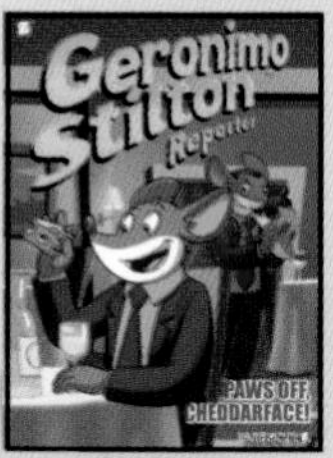
Geronimo Stilton
Reporter
PAWS OFF, CHEDDARFACE!

GERONIMO STILTON REPORTER #6
"Paws Off, Cheddarface!"

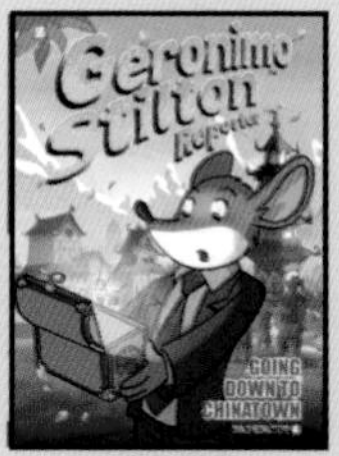
Geronimo Stilton
Reporter
GOING DOWN TO CHINATOWN

GERONIMO STILTON REPORTER #7
"Going Down to Chinatown"

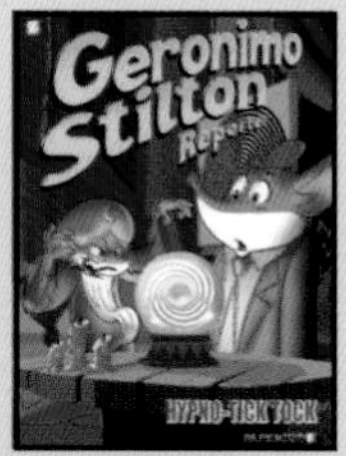
Geronimo Stilton
Reporter
HYPNO-TICK TOCK

GERONIMO STILTON REPORTER #8
"Hypno-Tick Tock"

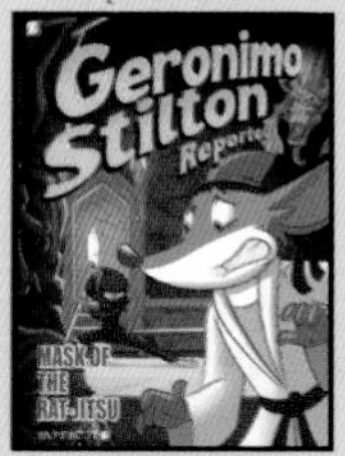
Geronimo Stilton
Reporter
MASK OF THE RAT-JITSU

GERONIMO STILTON REPORTER #9
"Mask of the Rat-Jitsu"

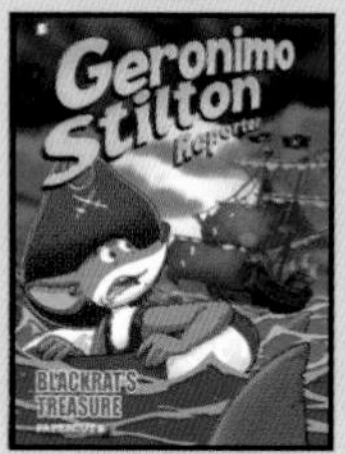
Geronimo Stilton
Reporter
BLACKRAT'S TREASURE

GERONIMO STILTON REPORTER #10
"Blackrat's Treasure"

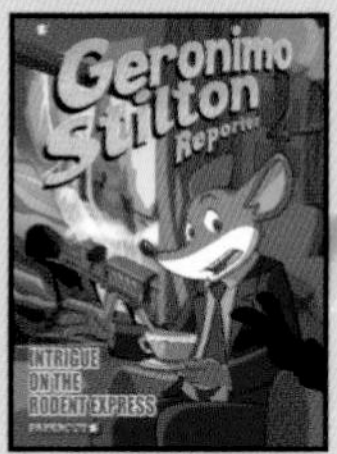
Geronimo Stilton
Reporter
INTRIGUE ON THE RODENT EXPRESS

GERONIMO STILTON REPORTER #11
"Intrigue on the Rodent Express"

...ALSO AVAILABLE WHEREVER E-BOOKS ARE SOLD!

See more at papercutz.com

Geronimo Stilton Reporter ™

#12 MOUSE HOUSE OF THE FUTURE
By Geronimo Stilton

PAPERCUTZ ™

NEW YORK

MOUSE HOUSE OF THE FUTURE
Geronimo Stilton names, characters and related indicia are copyright, trademark and exclusive license of Atlantyca S.p.A.
All right reserved.
The moral right of the author has been asserted.

Text by GERONIMO STILTON
Cover by ALESSANDRO MUSCILLO (artist) and CHRISTIAN ALIPRANDI (colorist)
Editorial supervision by ALESSANDRA BERELLO (Atlantyca S.p.A.)
Editing by ANITA DENTI (Atlantyca S.p.A.)
Script by DARIO SICCHIO
Art by ALESSANDRO MUSCILLO
Color by CHRISTIAN ALIPRANDI
Original Lettering by MARIA LETIZIA MIRABELLA

Special thanks to CARMEN CASTILLO

TM & © Atlantyca S.p.A. Animated Series © 2010 Atlantyca S.p.A.– All Rights Reserved
International Rights © Atlantyca S.p.A., Corso Magenta, 60/62 - 20123 Milano - Italia - foreignrights@atlantyca.it - www.atlantyca.com
© 2022 for this Work in English language by Papercutz, 160 Broadway, Suite 700, East Wing, New York, NY 10038
www.papercutz.com

Based on episode 12 of the Geronimo Stilton animated series "Casa, dolce casa! Davvero?," ["Mouse House of the Future"] written by TOM
MASON & DAN DANKO, storyboard by PIER DI GIÀ, LISA ARIOLI & PATRIZIA NASI
Preview based on episode 13 of the Geronimo Stilton animated series "Geronimo, Missione Africa!," ["Reported Missing"] written by
CATHERINE CUENA & PATRICK REGNARD, storyboard by PIER DI GIÀ, LISA ARIOLI & PATRIZIA NASI
www.geronimostilton.com

Stilton is the name of a famous English cheese. It is a registered trademark of the Stilton Cheesemakers' Association.
For more information go to www.stiltoncheese.co.uk

JAYJAY JACKSON — Production
WILSON RAMOS JR. & EMMA JENSEN— Lettering
TAKU WARD — Editorial Intern
INGRID RIOS — Editor
STEPHANIE BROOKS — Assistant Managing Editor
JIM SALICRUP
Editor-in-Chief

ISBN: 978-1-5458-0970-9

Printed in China
October 2022

Papercutz books may be purchased for business or promotional use.
For information on bulk purchases please contact
Macmillan Corporate and Premium Sales
Department at (800) 221-7945 x5442.

Distributed by Macmillan
First Papercutz Printing

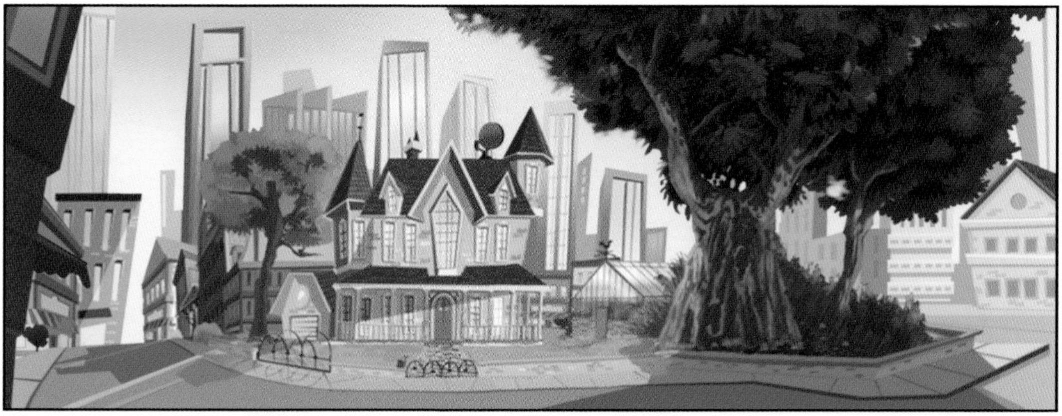

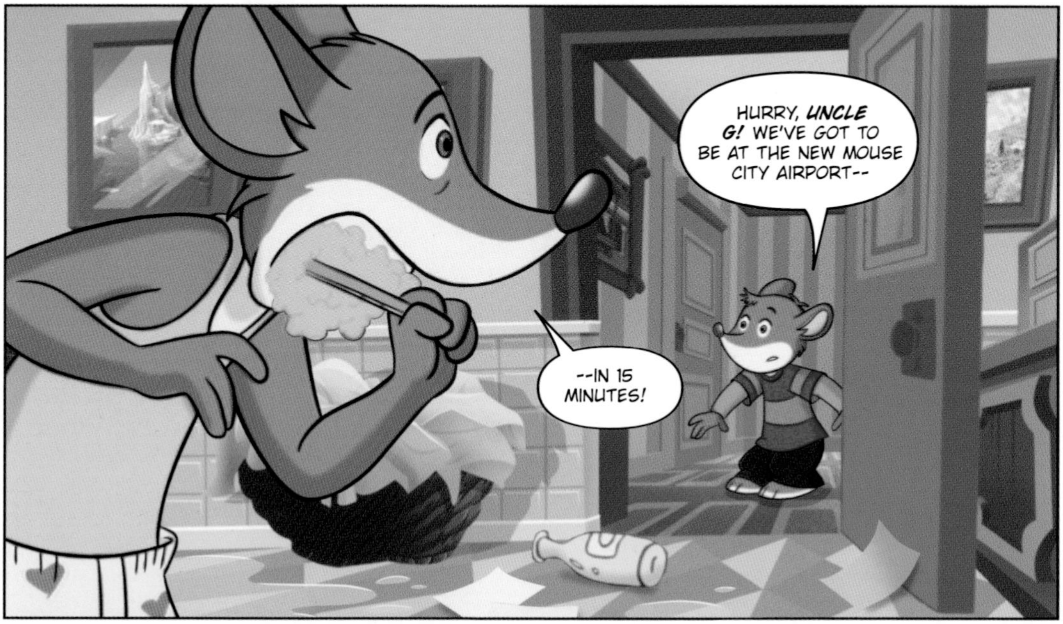
HURRY, UNCLE G! WE'VE GOT TO BE AT THE NEW MOUSE CITY AIRPORT--
--IN 15 MINUTES!

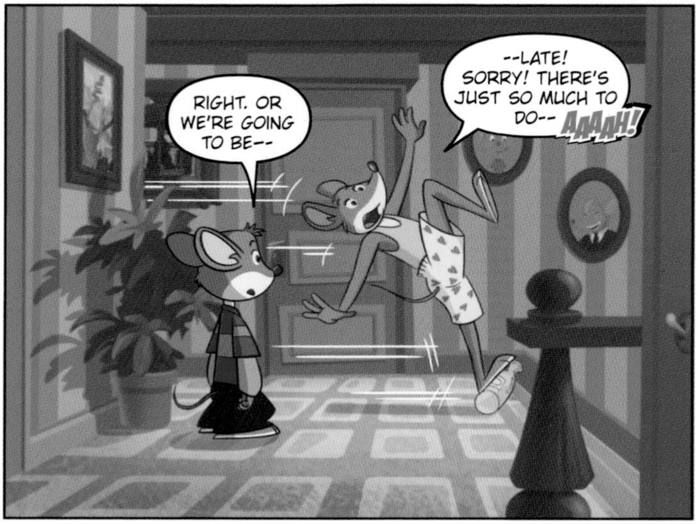
RIGHT. OR WE'RE GOING TO BE--
--LATE! SORRY! THERE'S JUST SO MUCH TO DO--
AAAAH!

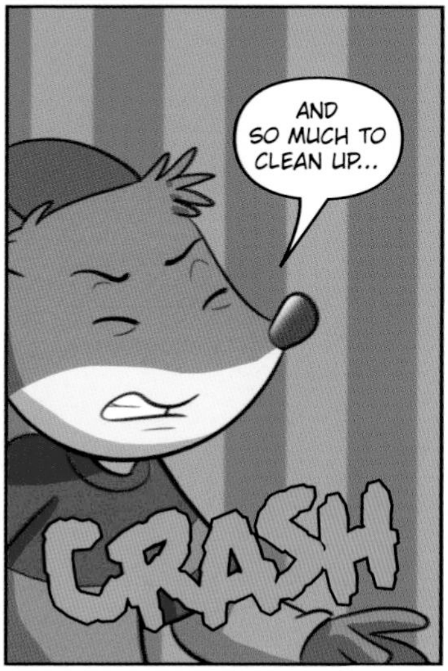
AND SO MUCH TO CLEAN UP...
CRASH

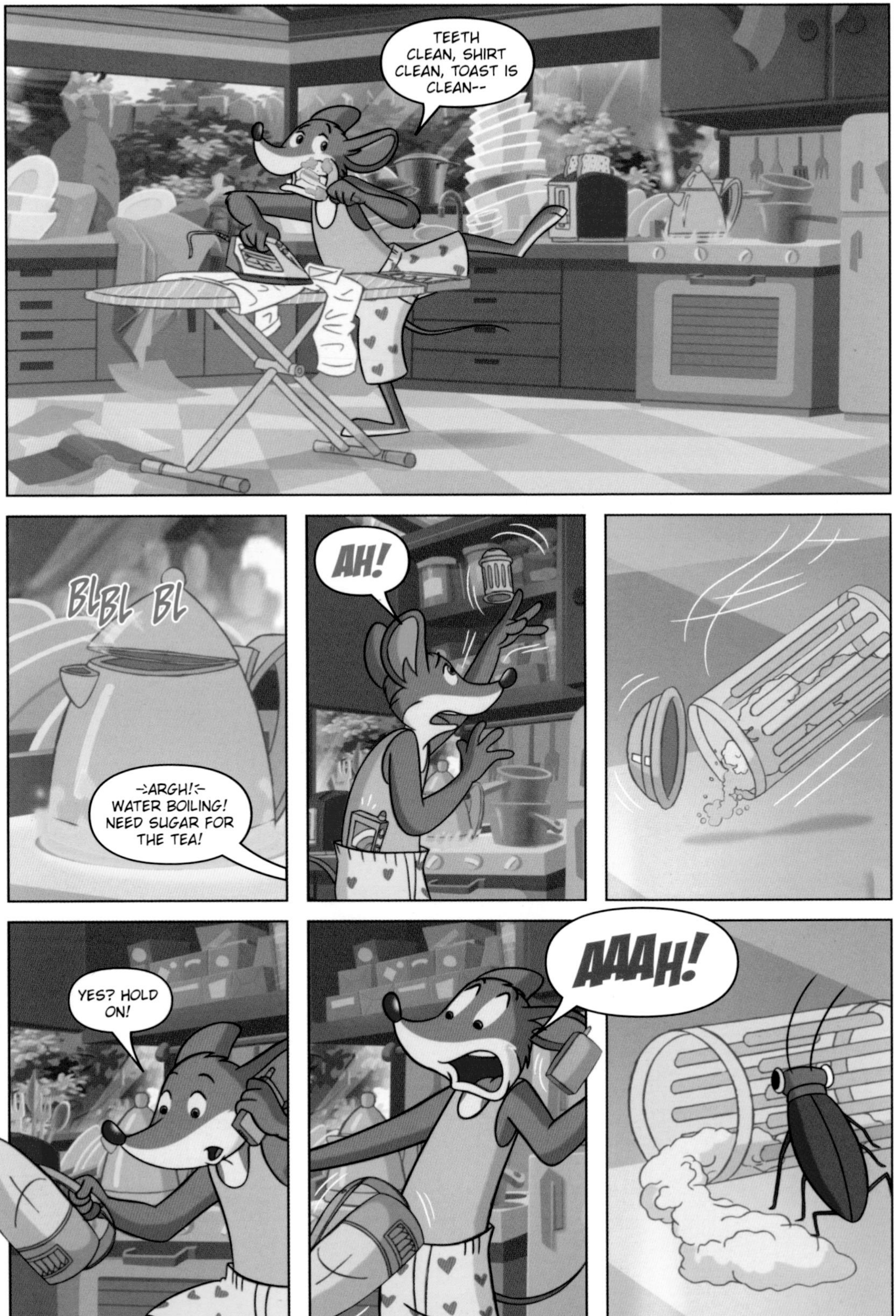
TEETH CLEAN, SHIRT CLEAN, TOAST IS CLEAN--
BLBL BL BL
-ARGH!- WATER BOILING! NEED SUGAR FOR THE TEA!
AH!
YES? HOLD ON!
AAAH!

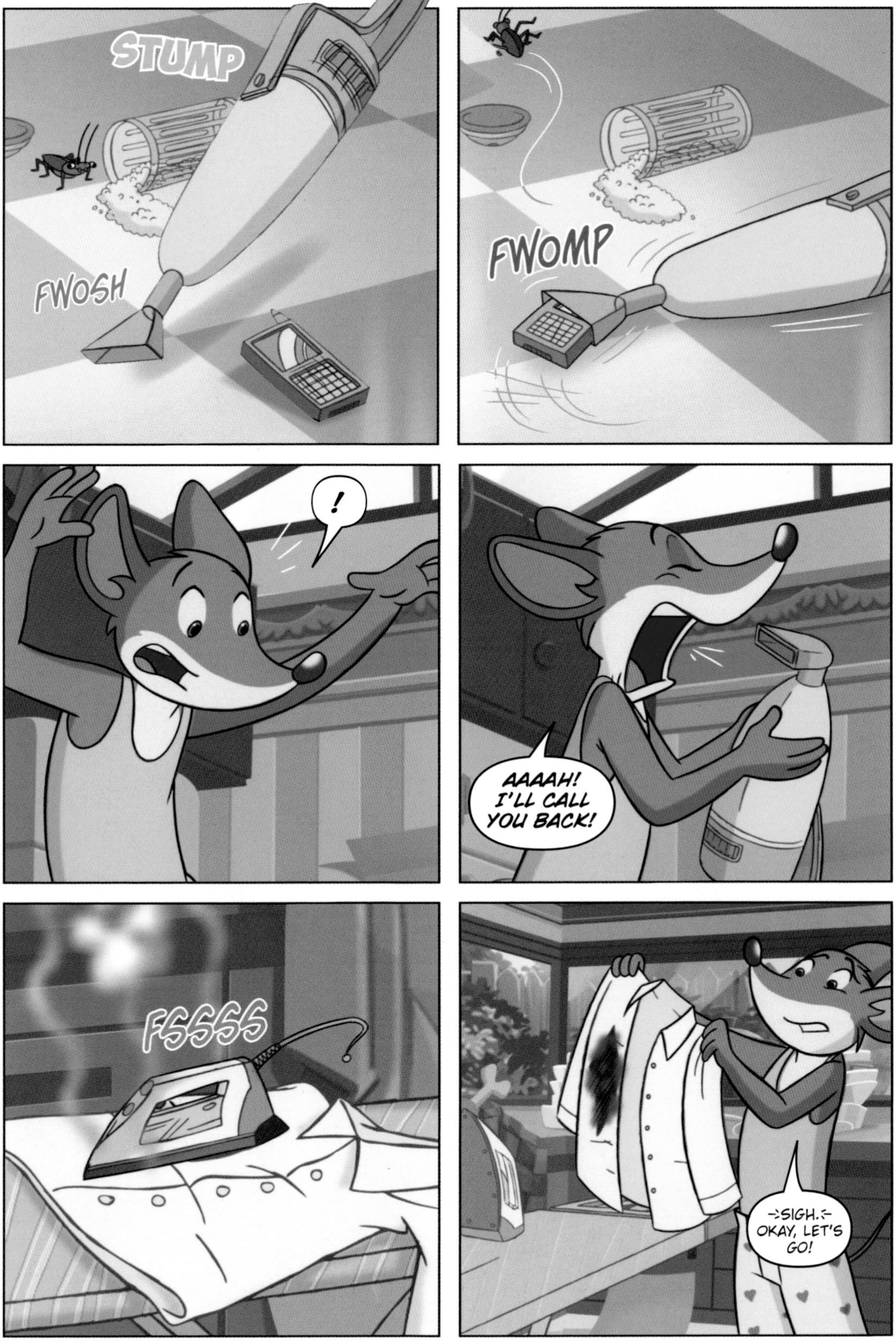
STUMP
FWOSH
FWOMP
!
AAAAH! I'LL CALL YOU BACK!
FSSSS
SIGH. OKAY, LET'S GO!

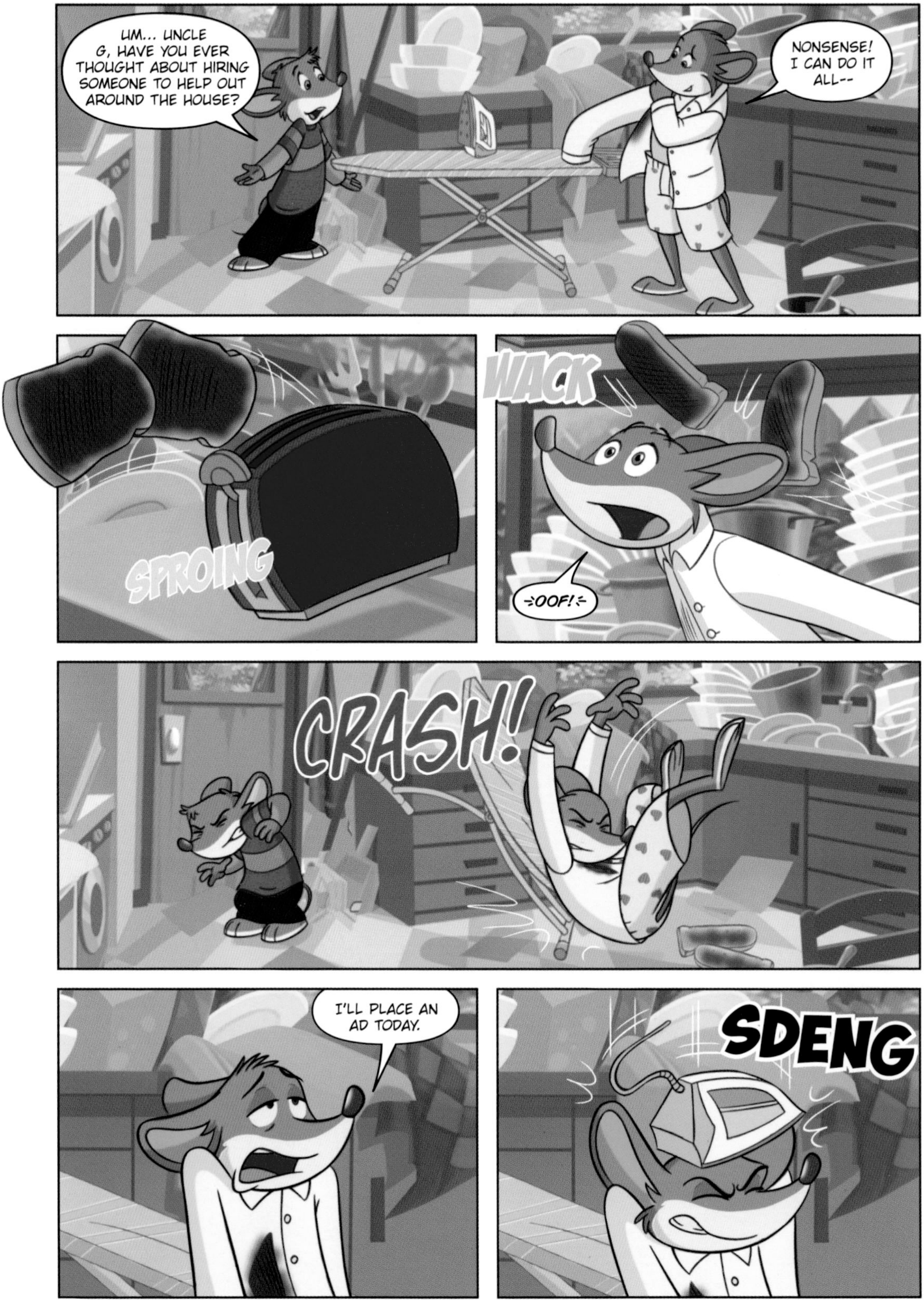
UM... UNCLE G, HAVE YOU EVER THOUGHT ABOUT HIRING SOMEONE TO HELP OUT AROUND THE HOUSE?
NONSENSE! I CAN DO IT ALL--
SPROING
WACK
OOF!
CRASH!
I'LL PLACE AN AD TODAY.
SDENG

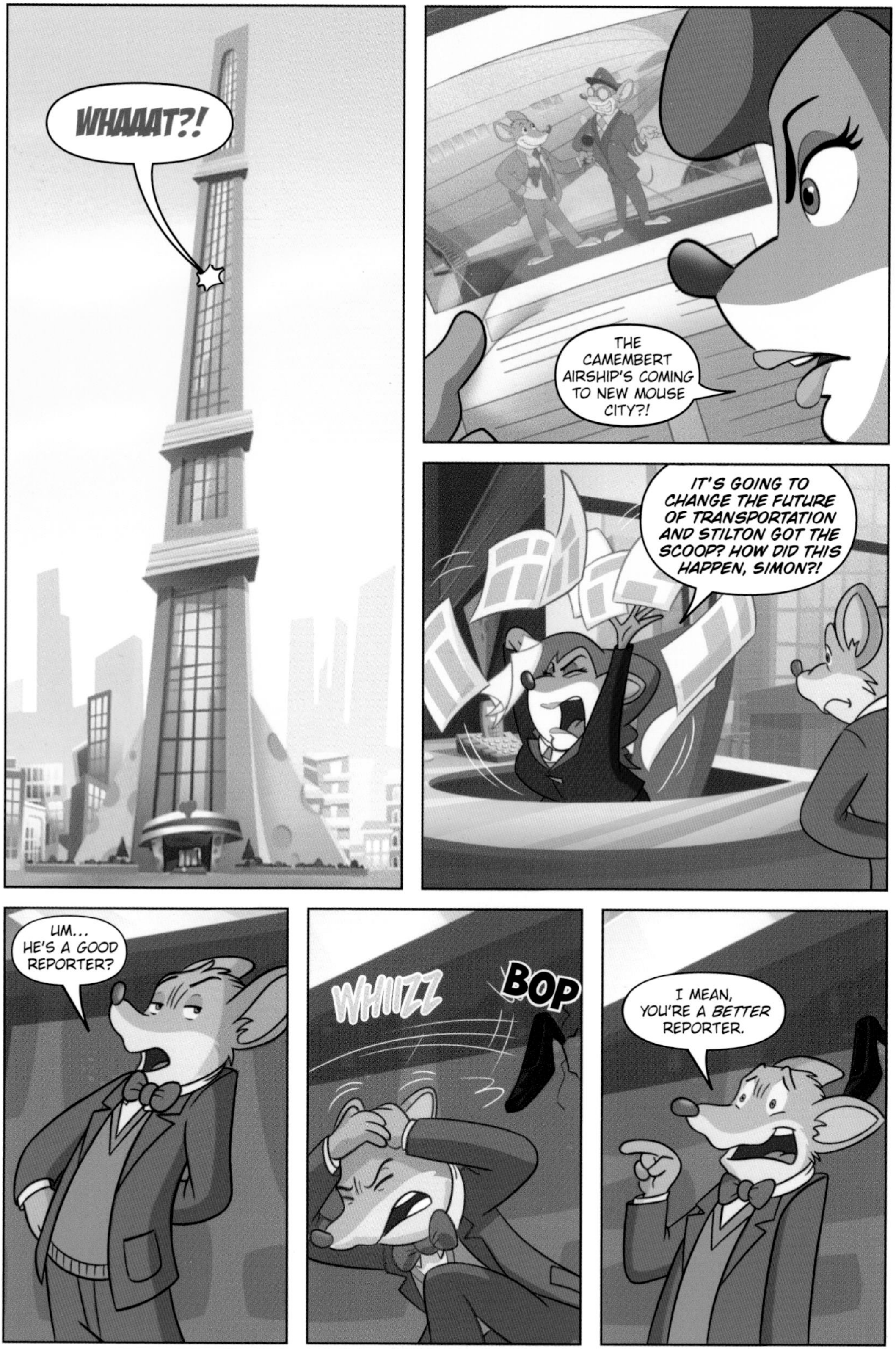
WHAAAT?!
THE CAMEMBERT AIRSHIP'S COMING TO NEW MOUSE CITY?!
IT'S GOING TO CHANGE THE FUTURE OF TRANSPORTATION AND STILTON GOT THE SCOOP? HOW DID THIS HAPPEN, SIMON?!
UM... HE'S A GOOD REPORTER?
WHIIZZ
BOP
I MEAN, YOU'RE A *BETTER* REPORTER.

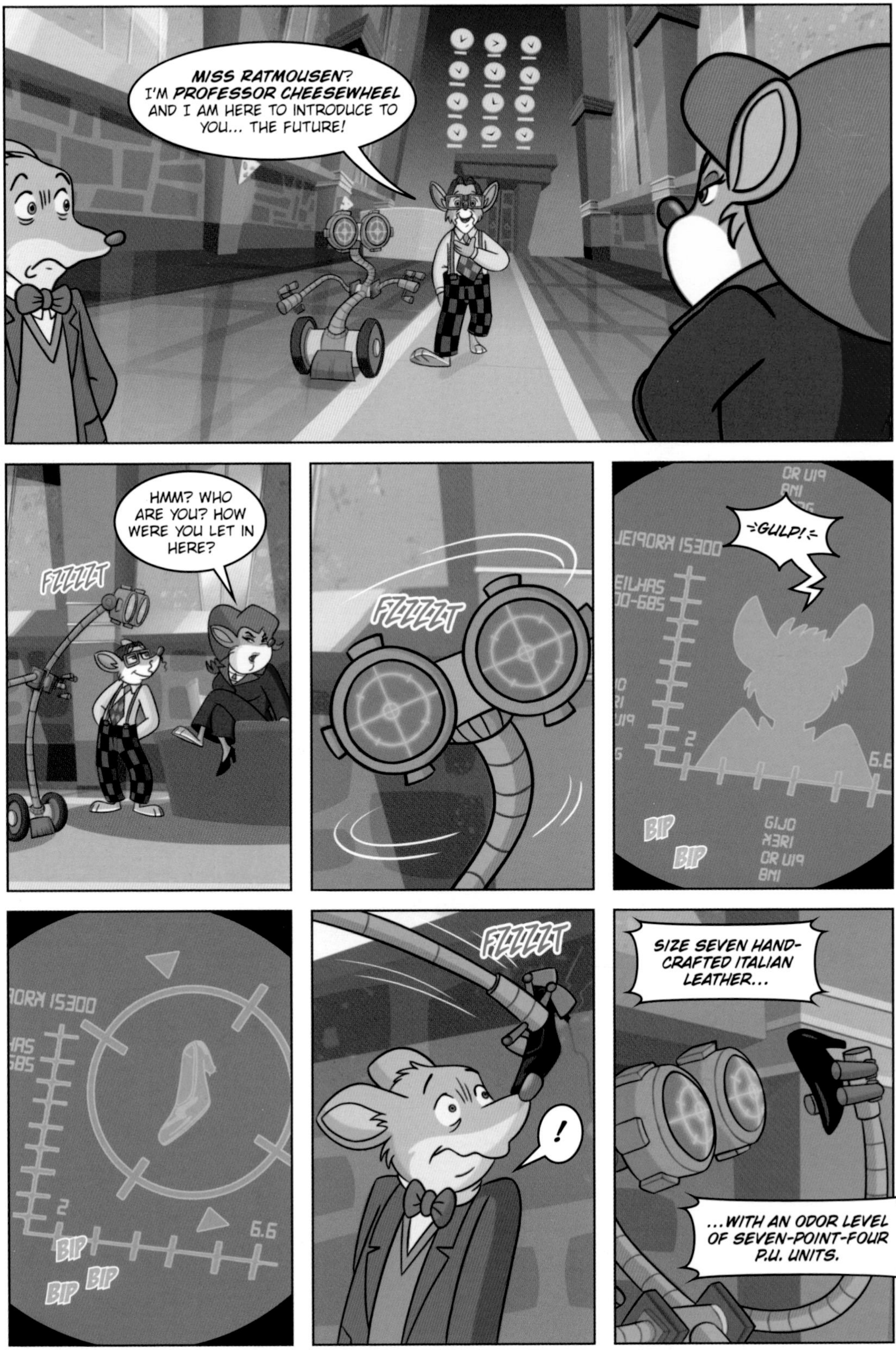
MISS RATMOUSEN? I'M PROFESSOR CHEESEWHEEL AND I AM HERE TO INTRODUCE TO YOU... THE FUTURE!
HMM? WHO ARE YOU? HOW WERE YOU LET IN HERE?
FZZZZT
FZZZZT
GULP!
BIP
BIP
BIP
BIP
BIP
FZZZZT
!
SIZE SEVEN HAND-CRAFTED ITALIAN LEATHER...
...WITH AN ODOR LEVEL OF SEVEN-POINT-FOUR P.U. UNITS.

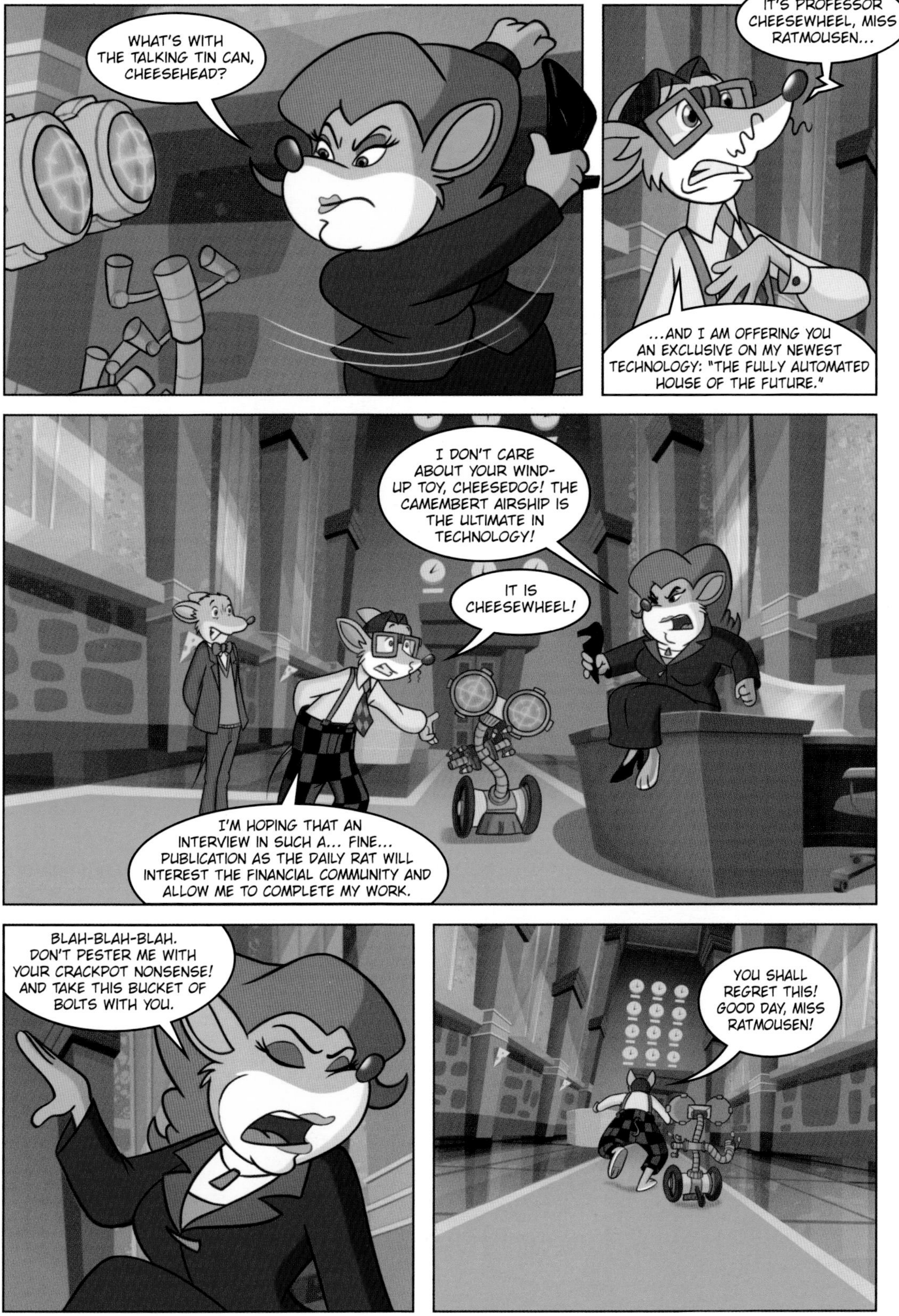
WHAT'S WITH THE TALKING TIN CAN, CHEESEHEAD?
IT'S PROFESSOR CHEESEWHEEL, MISS RATMOUSEN...
...AND I AM OFFERING YOU AN EXCLUSIVE ON MY NEWEST TECHNOLOGY: "THE FULLY AUTOMATED HOUSE OF THE FUTURE."
I DON'T CARE ABOUT YOUR WIND-UP TOY, CHEESEDOG! THE CAMEMBERT AIRSHIP IS THE ULTIMATE IN TECHNOLOGY!
IT IS CHEESEWHEEL!
I'M HOPING THAT AN INTERVIEW IN SUCH A... FINE... PUBLICATION AS THE DAILY RAT WILL INTEREST THE FINANCIAL COMMUNITY AND ALLOW ME TO COMPLETE MY WORK.
BLAH-BLAH-BLAH. DON'T PESTER ME WITH YOUR CRACKPOT NONSENSE! AND TAKE THIS BUCKET OF BOLTS WITH YOU.
YOU SHALL REGRET THIS! GOOD DAY, MISS RATMOUSEN!

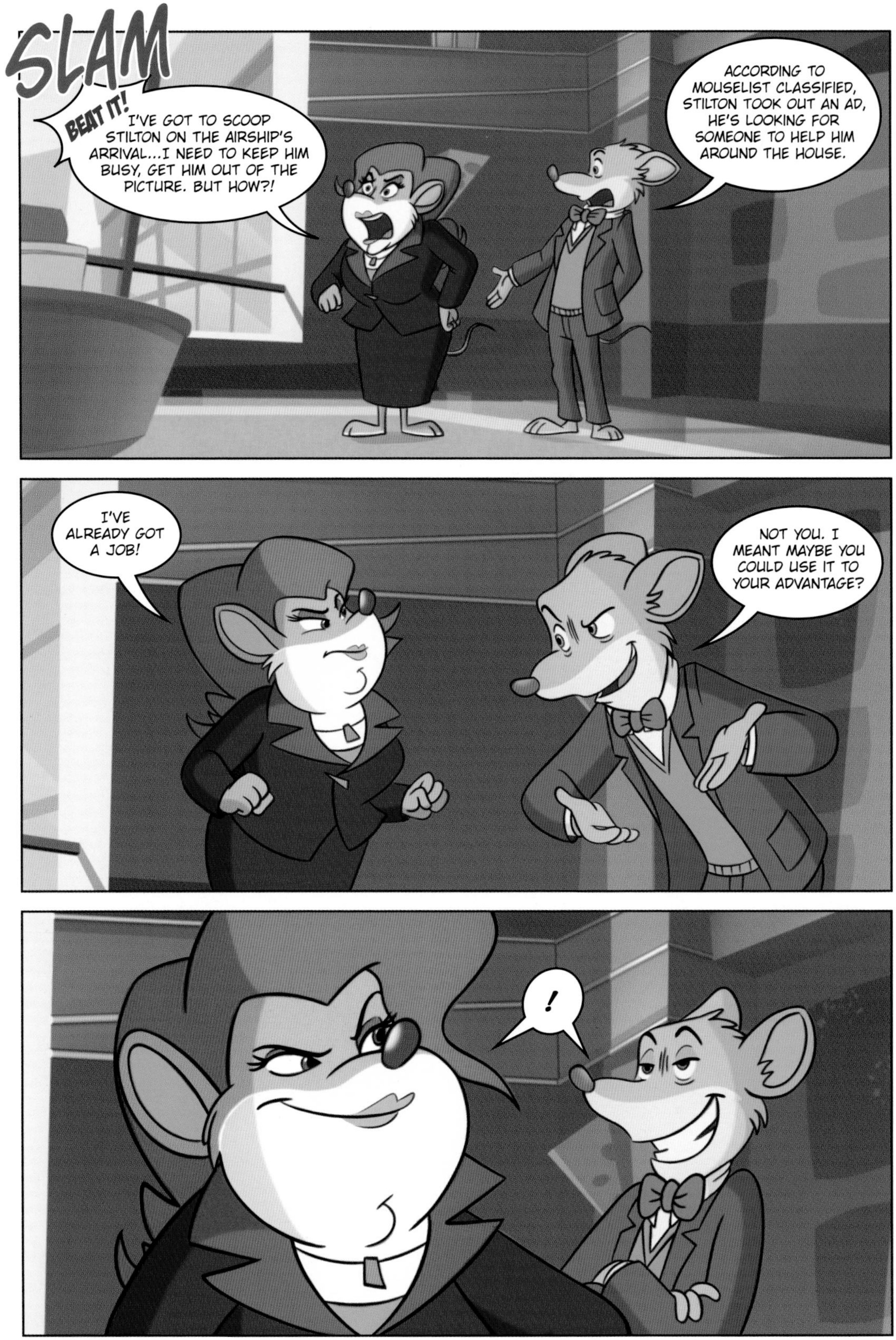
SLAM
BEAT IT!
I'VE GOT TO SCOOP STILTON ON THE AIRSHIP'S ARRIVAL...I NEED TO KEEP HIM BUSY, GET HIM OUT OF THE PICTURE. BUT HOW?!
ACCORDING TO MOUSELIST CLASSIFIED, STILTON TOOK OUT AN AD, HE'S LOOKING FOR SOMEONE TO HELP HIM AROUND THE HOUSE.
I'VE ALREADY GOT A JOB!
NOT YOU. I MEANT MAYBE YOU COULD USE IT TO YOUR ADVANTAGE?
!

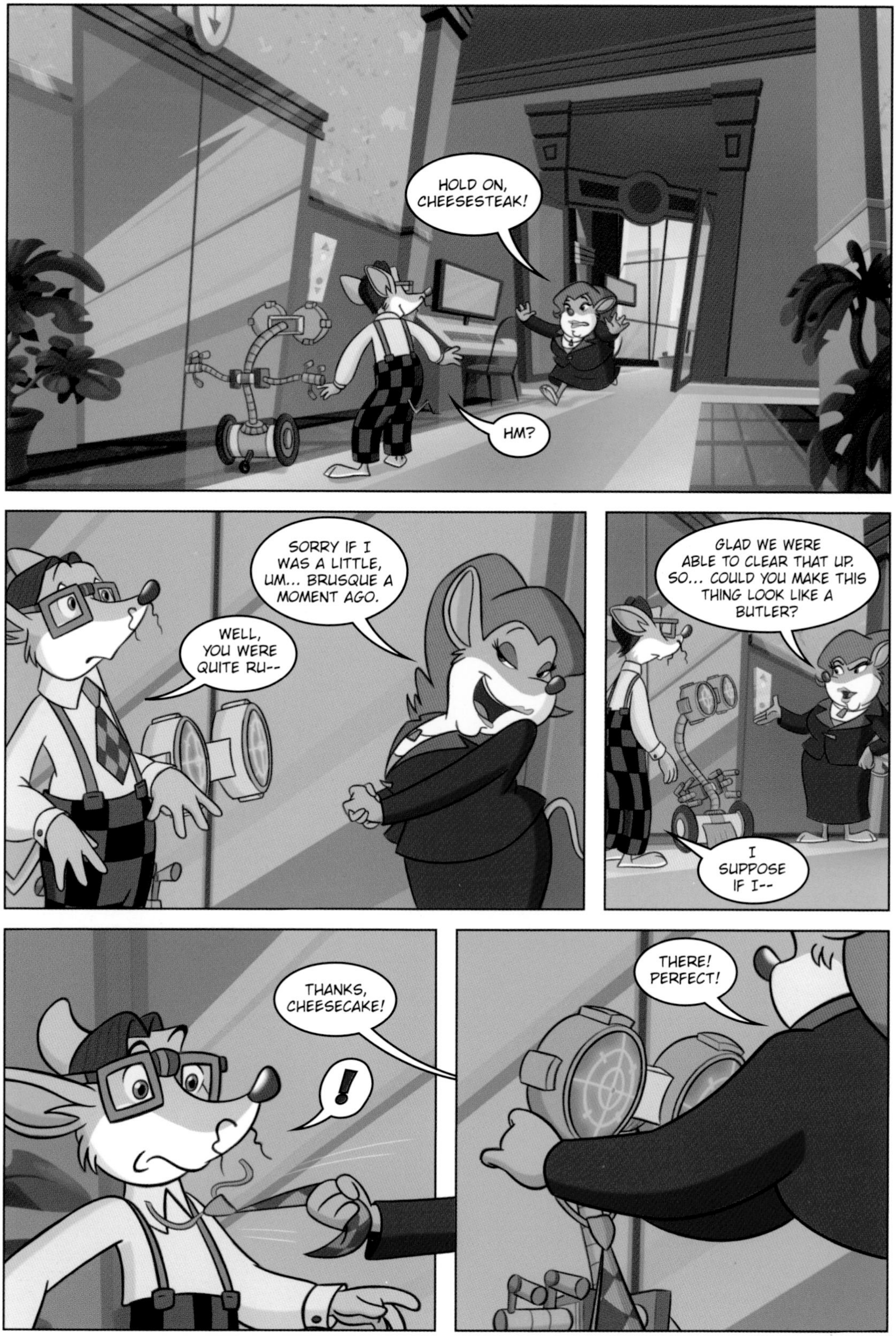
HOLD ON, CHEESESTEAK!
HM?
SORRY IF I WAS A LITTLE, UM... BRUSQUE A MOMENT AGO.
WELL, YOU WERE QUITE RU--
GLAD WE WERE ABLE TO CLEAR THAT UP. SO... COULD YOU MAKE THIS THING LOOK LIKE A BUTLER?
I SUPPOSE IF I--
THANKS, CHEESECAKE!
!
THERE! PERFECT!

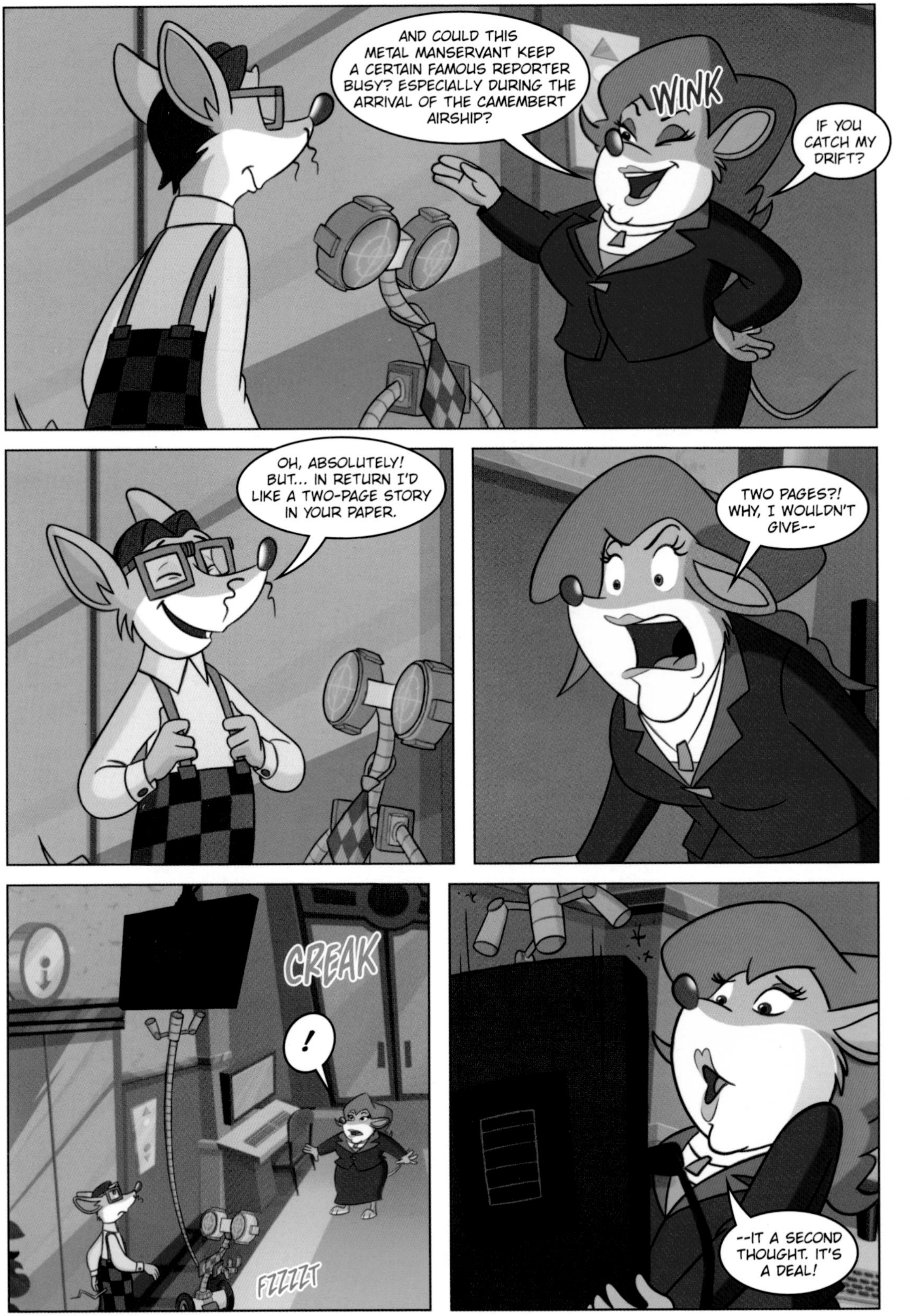
AND COULD THIS METAL MANSERVANT KEEP A CERTAIN FAMOUS REPORTER BUSY? ESPECIALLY DURING THE ARRIVAL OF THE CAMEMBERT AIRSHIP?
WINK
IF YOU CATCH MY DRIFT?
OH, ABSOLUTELY! BUT... IN RETURN I'D LIKE A TWO-PAGE STORY IN YOUR PAPER.
TWO PAGES?! WHY, I WOULDN'T GIVE--
CREAK
!
FZZZZT
--IT A SECOND THOUGHT. IT'S A DEAL!

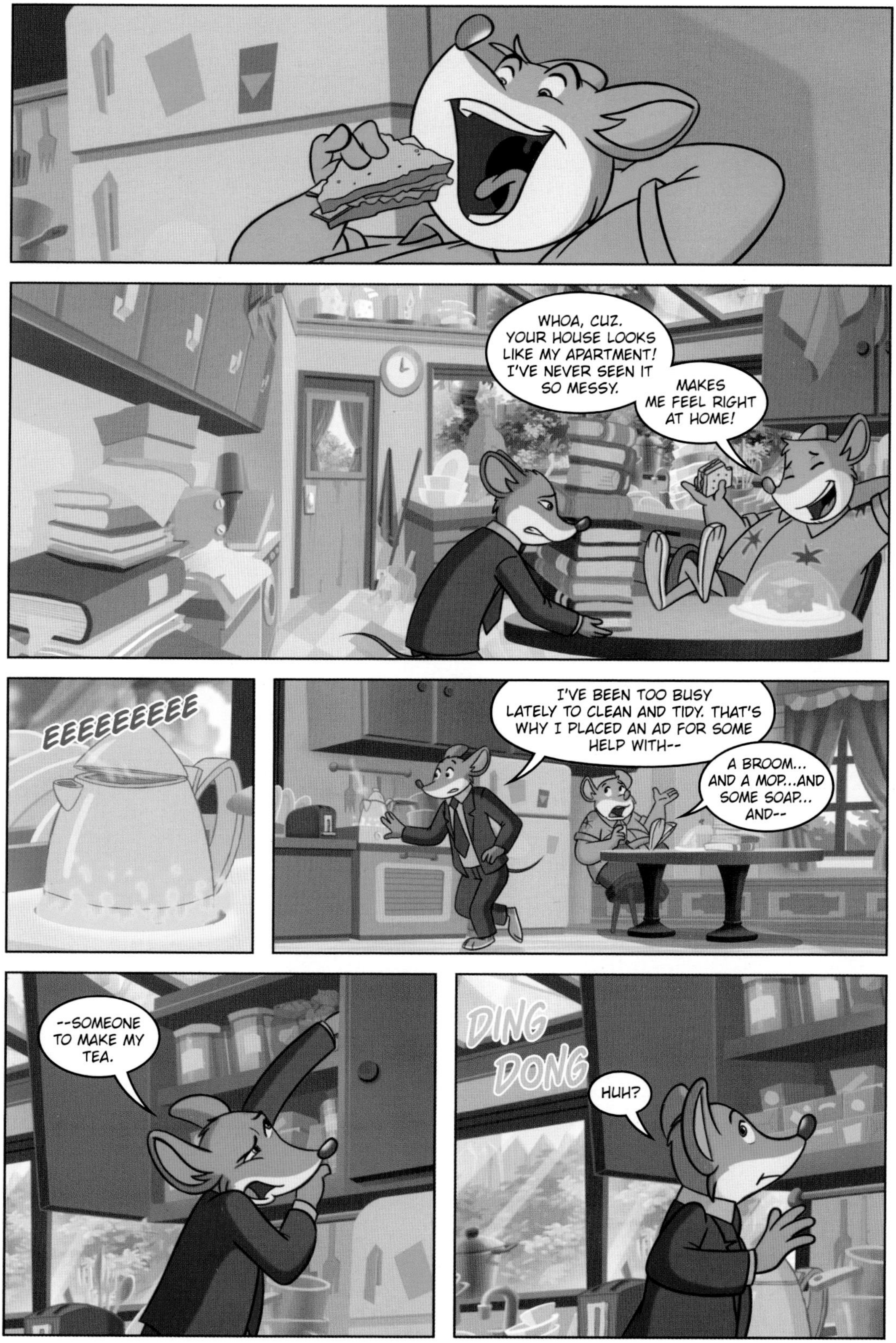
WHOA, CUZ. YOUR HOUSE LOOKS LIKE MY APARTMENT! I'VE NEVER SEEN IT SO MESSY.
MAKES ME FEEL RIGHT AT HOME!
EEEEEEEEE
I'VE BEEN TOO BUSY LATELY TO CLEAN AND TIDY. THAT'S WHY I PLACED AN AD FOR SOME HELP WITH--
A BROOM... AND A MOP...AND SOME SOAP... AND--
--SOMEONE TO MAKE MY TEA.
DING DONG
HUH?

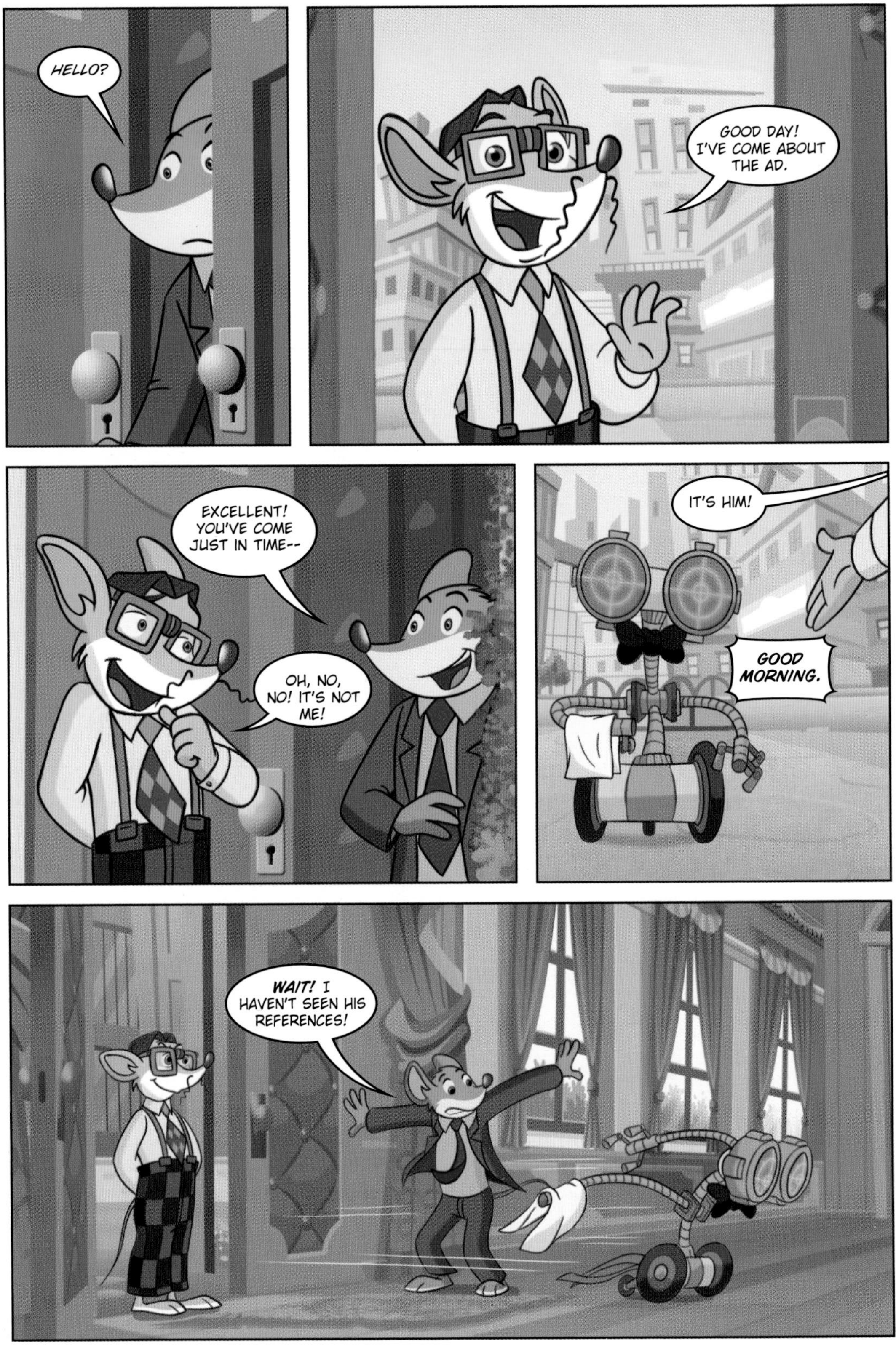

HELLO?
GOOD DAY! I'VE COME ABOUT THE AD.
EXCELLENT! YOU'VE COME JUST IN TIME--
OH, NO, NO! IT'S NOT ME!
IT'S HIM!
GOOD MORNING.
WAIT! I HAVEN'T SEEN HIS REFERENCES!

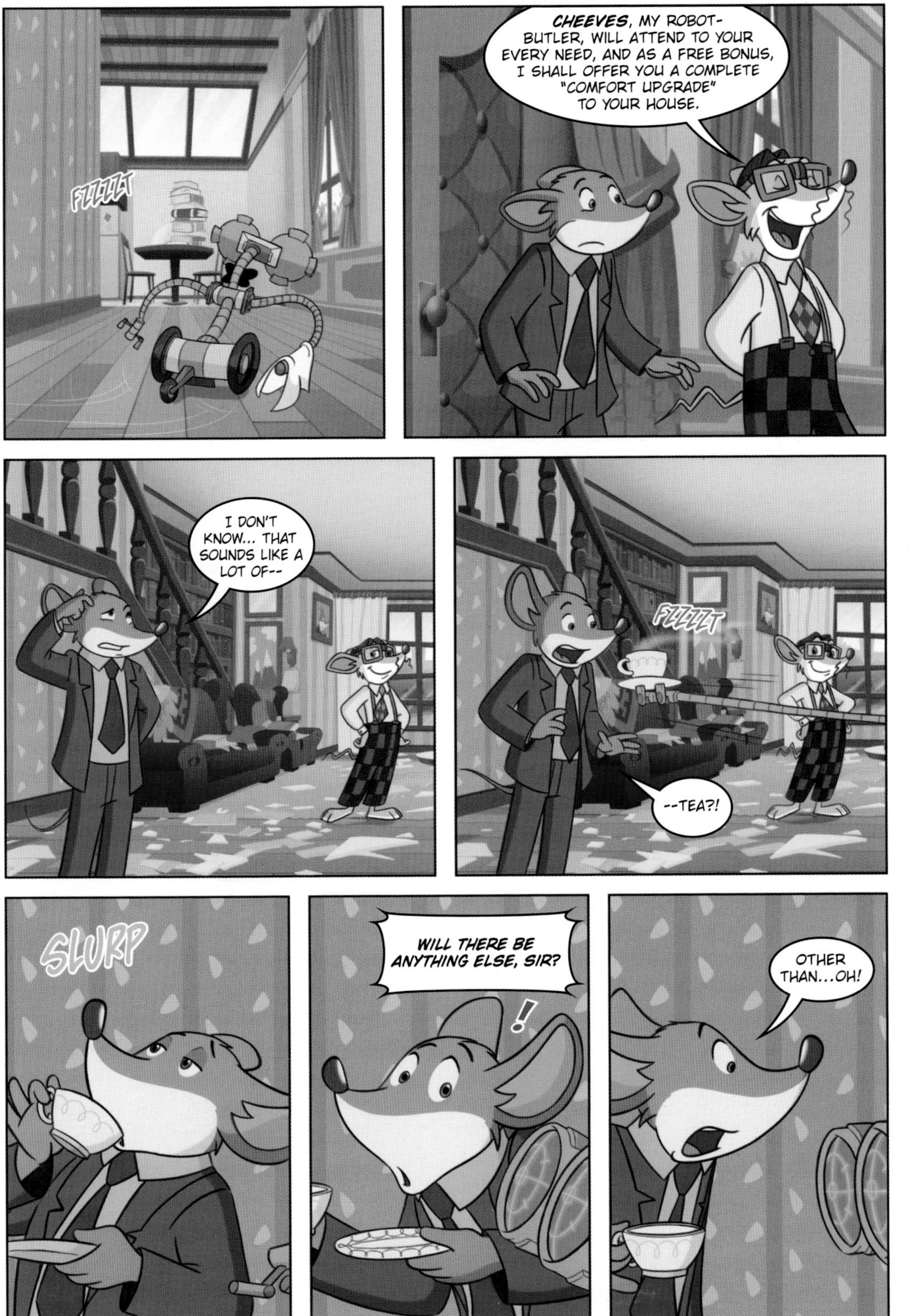
FZZZZT
CHEEVES, MY ROBOT-BUTLER, WILL ATTEND TO YOUR EVERY NEED, AND AS A FREE BONUS, I SHALL OFFER YOU A COMPLETE "COMFORT UPGRADE" TO YOUR HOUSE.
I DON'T KNOW... THAT SOUNDS LIKE A LOT OF--
FZZZZZT
--TEA?!
SLURP
WILL THERE BE ANYTHING ELSE, SIR?
!
OTHER THAN...OH!

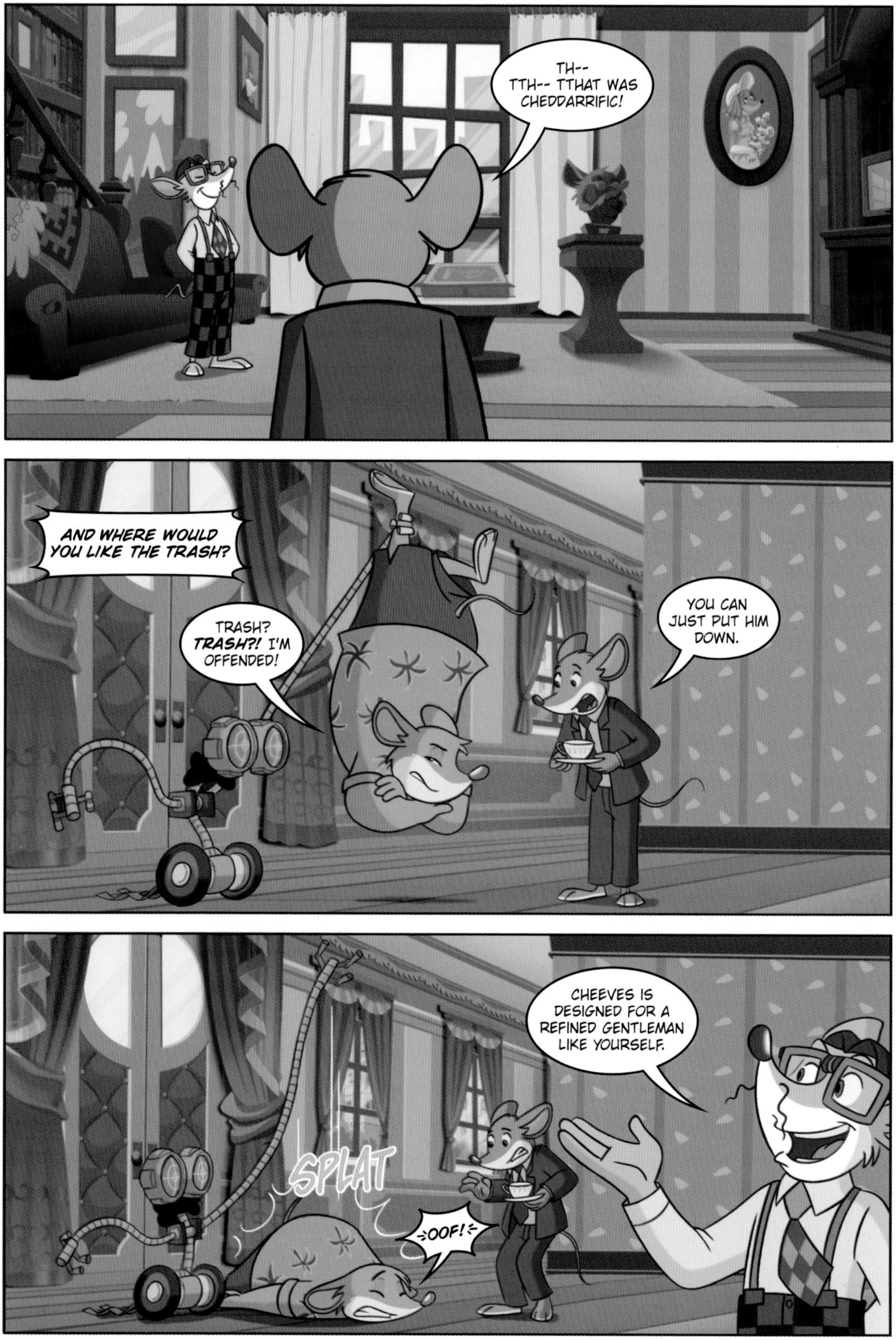
TH--
TTH-- TTHAT WAS CHEDDARRIFIC!
AND WHERE WOULD YOU LIKE THE TRASH?
TRASH? TRASH?! I'M OFFENDED!
YOU CAN JUST PUT HIM DOWN.
SPLAT
OOF!
CHEEVES IS DESIGNED FOR A REFINED GENTLEMAN LIKE YOURSELF.

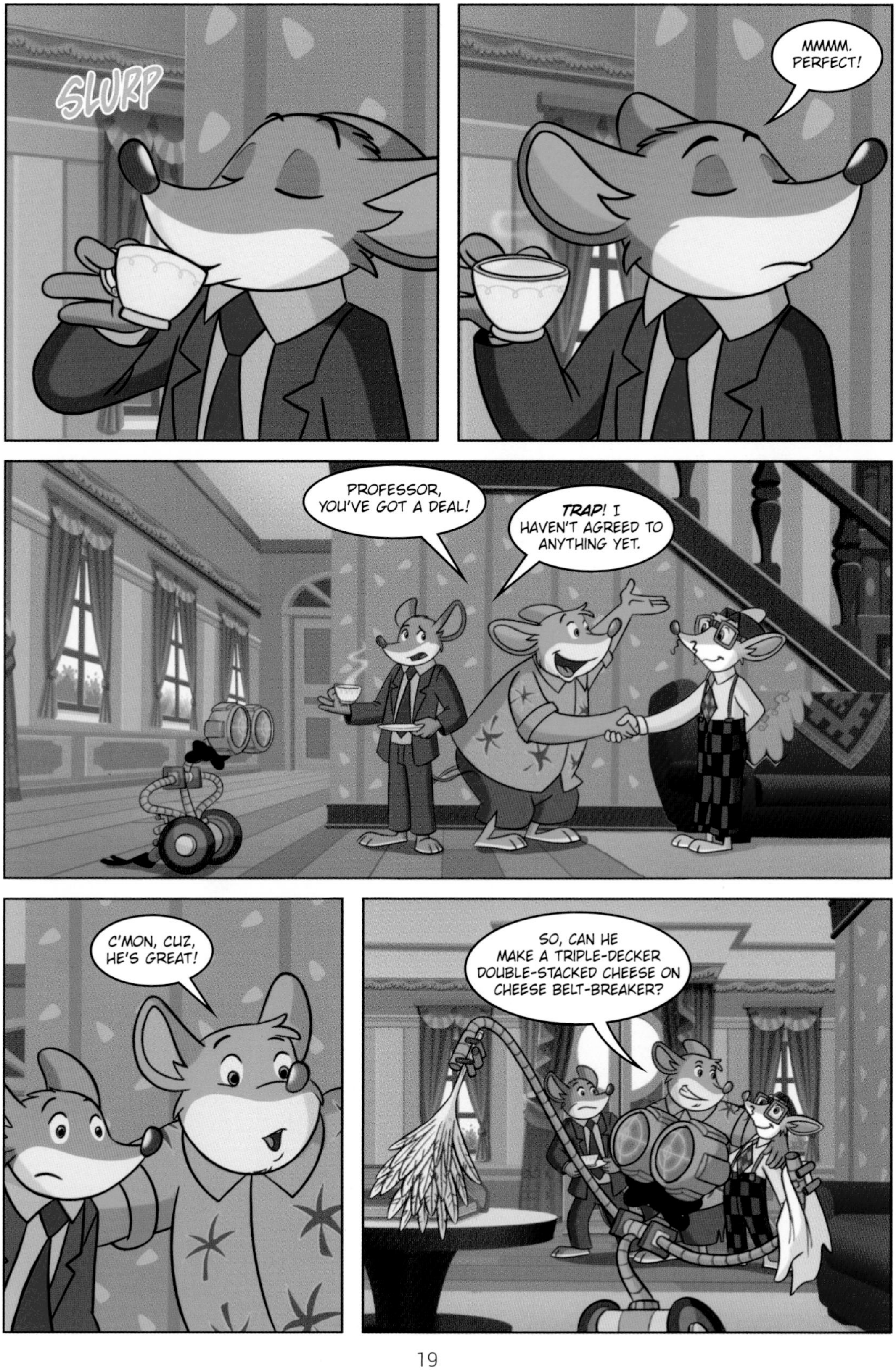
SLURP
MMMM. PERFECT!
PROFESSOR, YOU'VE GOT A DEAL!
TRAP! I HAVEN'T AGREED TO ANYTHING YET.
C'MON, CUZ, HE'S GREAT!
SO, CAN HE MAKE A TRIPLE-DECKER DOUBLE-STACKED CHEESE ON CHEESE BELT-BREAKER?

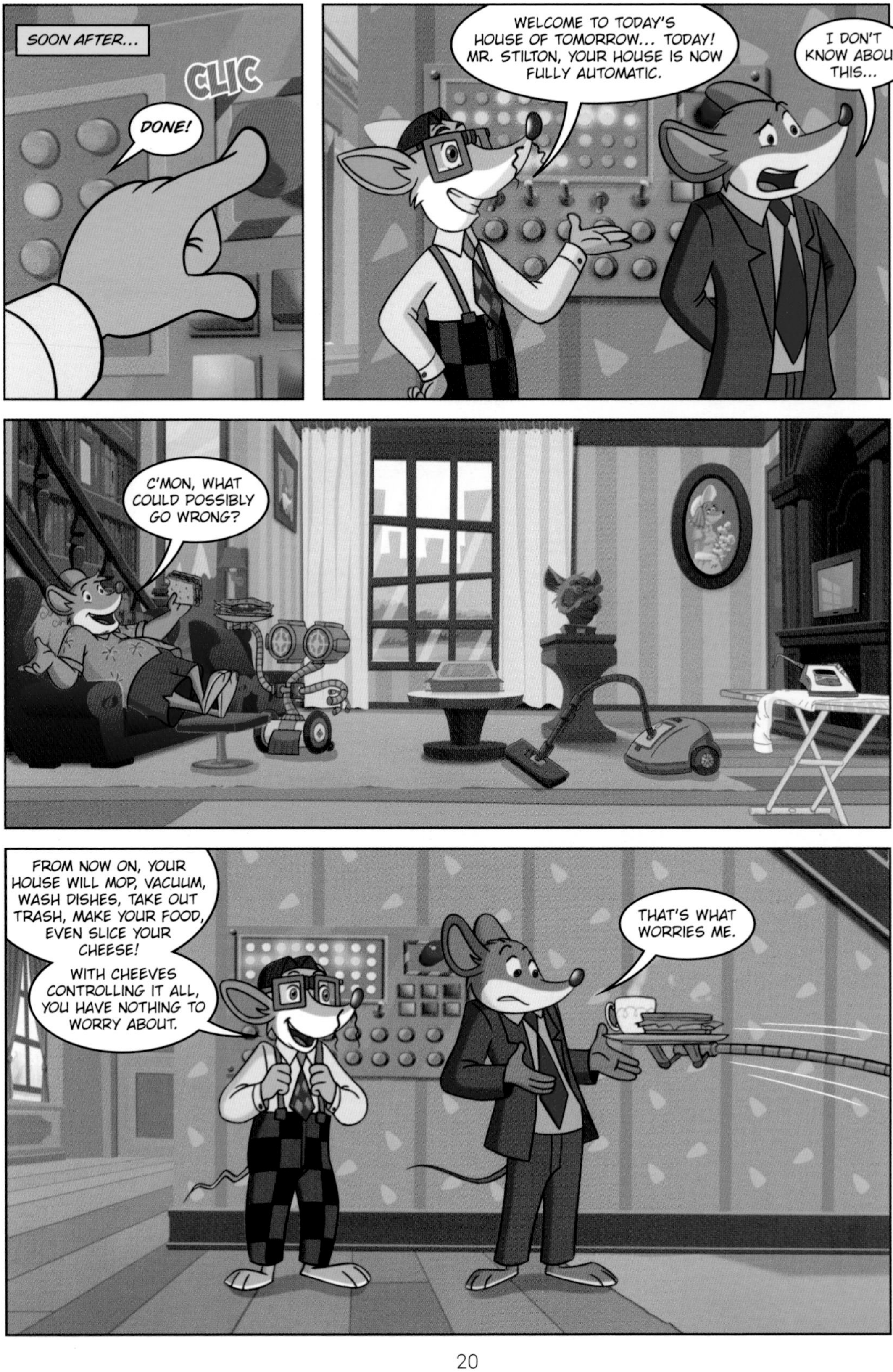
SOON AFTER...
CLIC
DONE!
WELCOME TO TODAY'S HOUSE OF TOMORROW... TODAY! MR. STILTON, YOUR HOUSE IS NOW FULLY AUTOMATIC.
I DON'T KNOW ABOUT THIS...
C'MON, WHAT COULD POSSIBLY GO WRONG?
FROM NOW ON, YOUR HOUSE WILL MOP, VACUUM, WASH DISHES, TAKE OUT TRASH, MAKE YOUR FOOD, EVEN SLICE YOUR CHEESE!
WITH CHEEVES CONTROLLING IT ALL, YOU HAVE NOTHING TO WORRY ABOUT.
THAT'S WHAT WORRIES ME.

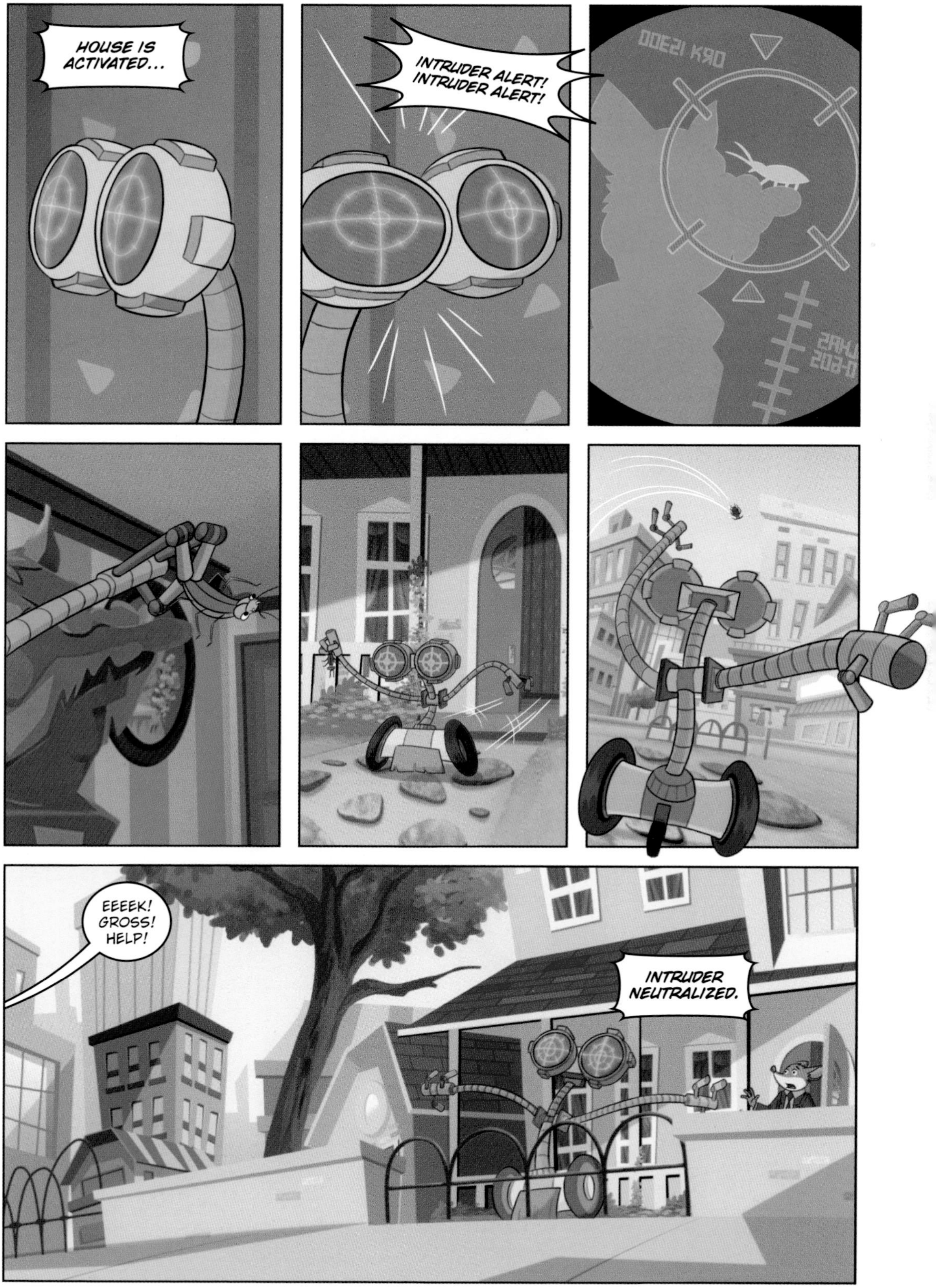
HOUSE IS ACTIVATED...
INTRUDER ALERT! INTRUDER ALERT!
EEEEK! GROSS! HELP!
INTRUDER NEUTRALIZED.

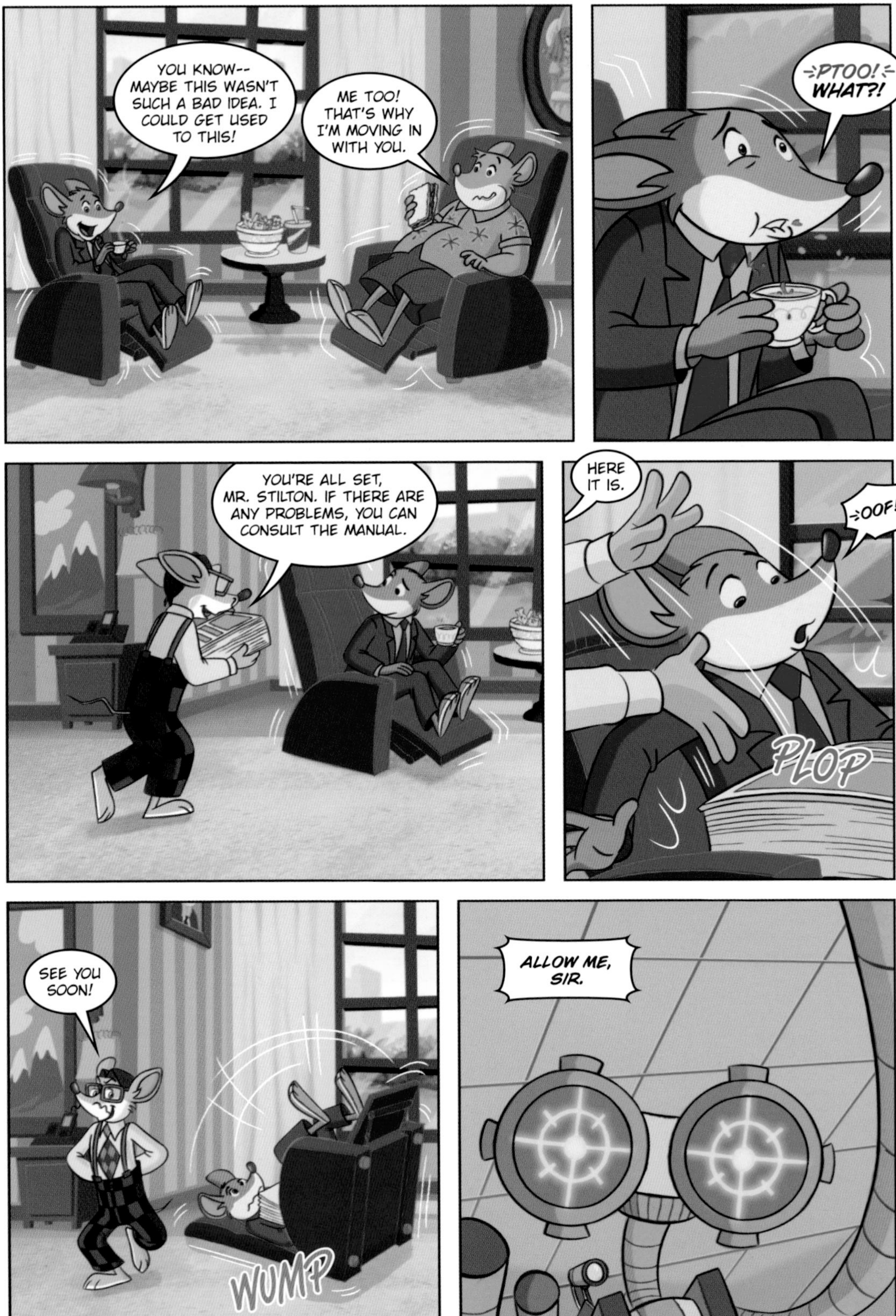
YOU KNOW-- MAYBE THIS WASN'T SUCH A BAD IDEA. I COULD GET USED TO THIS!
ME TOO! THAT'S WHY I'M MOVING IN WITH YOU.
PTOO! WHAT?!
YOU'RE ALL SET, MR. STILTON. IF THERE ARE ANY PROBLEMS, YOU CAN CONSULT THE MANUAL.
HERE IT IS.
OOF!
PLOP
SEE YOU SOON!
WUMP
ALLOW ME, SIR.

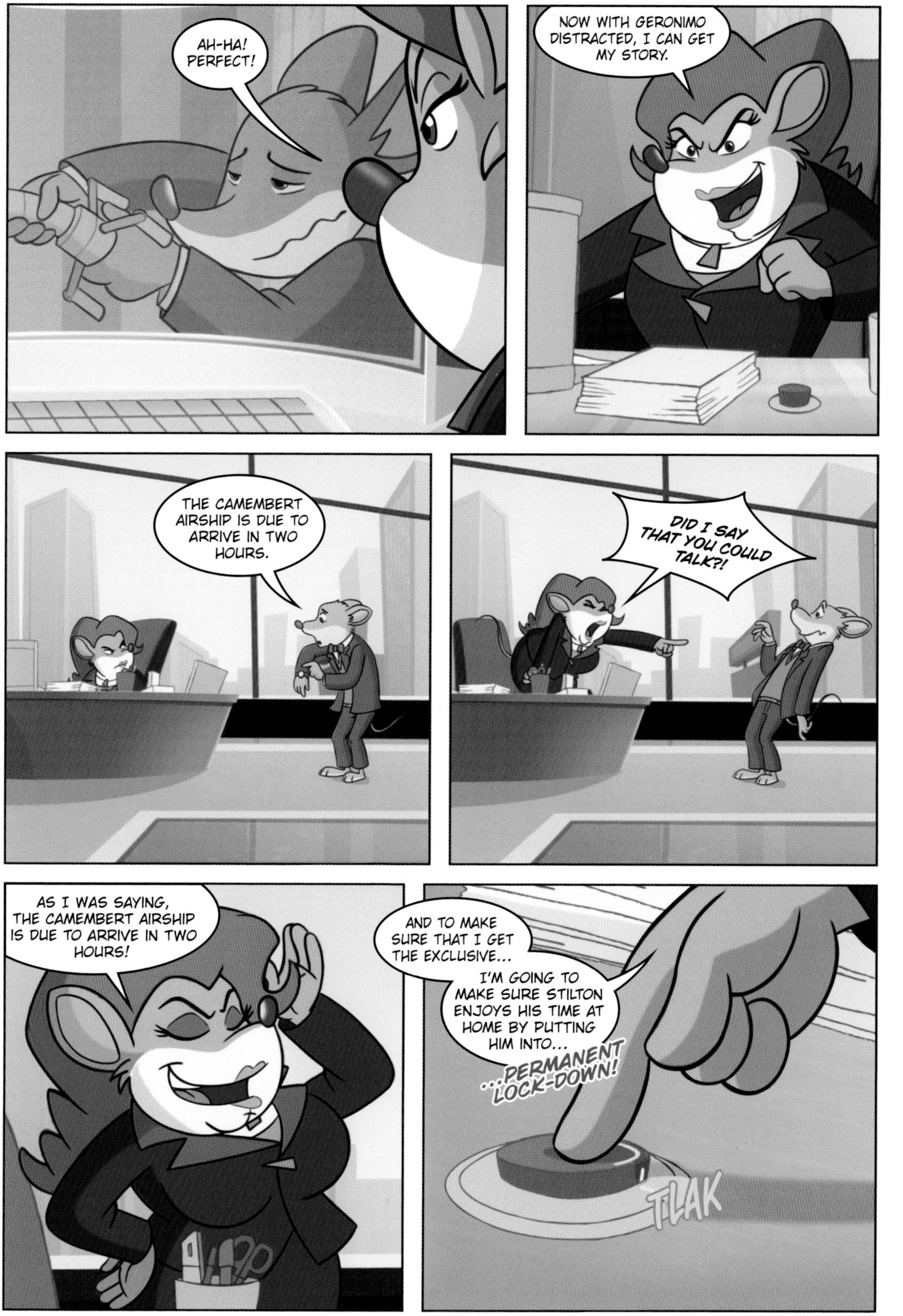
AH-HA! PERFECT!
NOW WITH GERONIMO DISTRACTED, I CAN GET MY STORY.
THE CAMEMBERT AIRSHIP IS DUE TO ARRIVE IN TWO HOURS.
DID I SAY THAT YOU COULD TALK?!
AS I WAS SAYING, THE CAMEMBERT AIRSHIP IS DUE TO ARRIVE IN TWO HOURS!
AND TO MAKE SURE THAT I GET THE EXCLUSIVE...
I'M GOING TO MAKE SURE STILTON ENJOYS HIS TIME AT HOME BY PUTTING HIM INTO...
...PERMANENT LOCK-DOWN!
TLAK

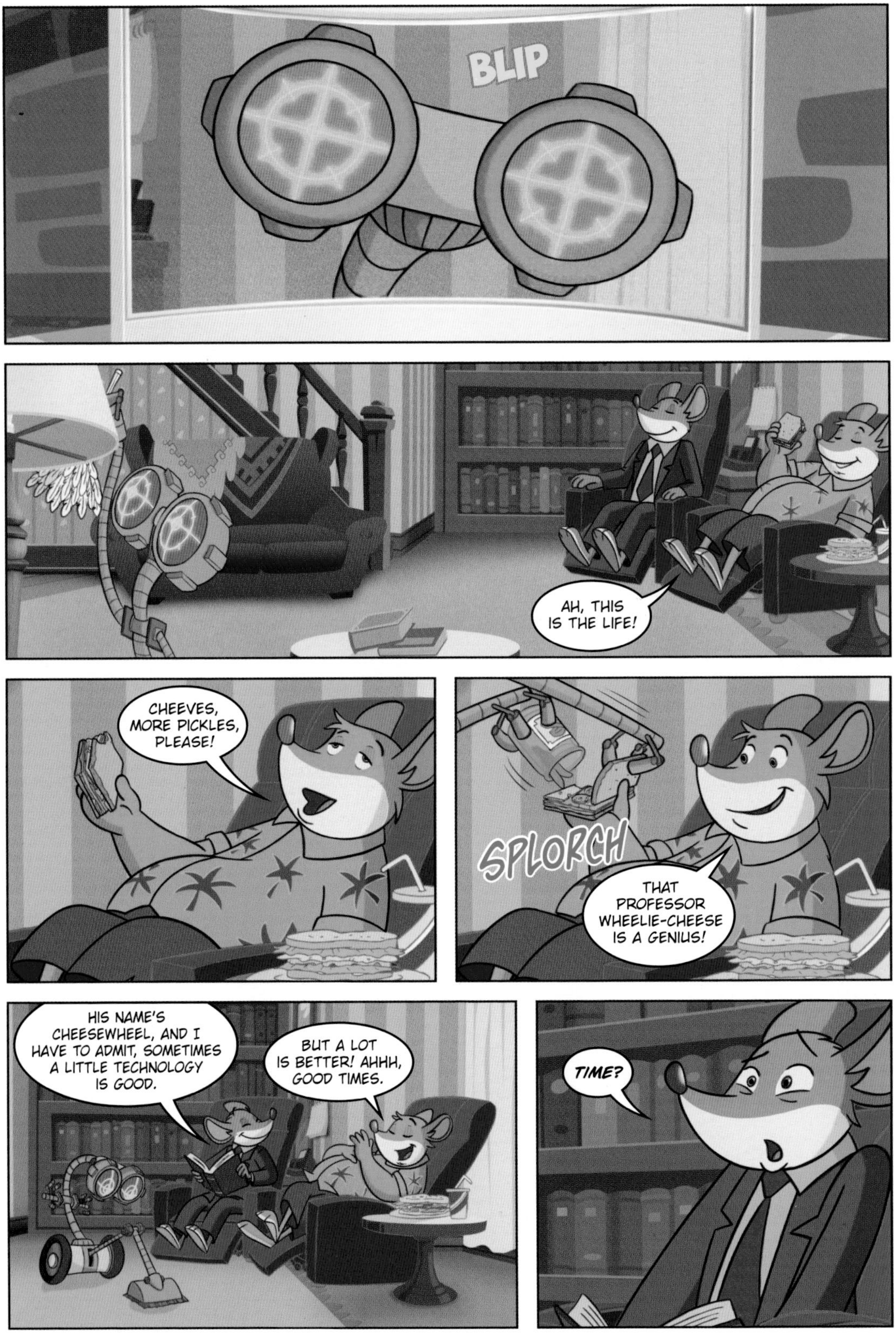
BLIP
AH, THIS IS THE LIFE!
CHEEVES, MORE PICKLES, PLEASE!
SPLORCH
THAT PROFESSOR WHEELIE-CHEESE IS A GENIUS!
HIS NAME'S CHEESEWHEEL, AND I HAVE TO ADMIT, SOMETIMES A LITTLE TECHNOLOGY IS GOOD.
BUT A LOT IS BETTER! AHHH, GOOD TIMES.
TIME?

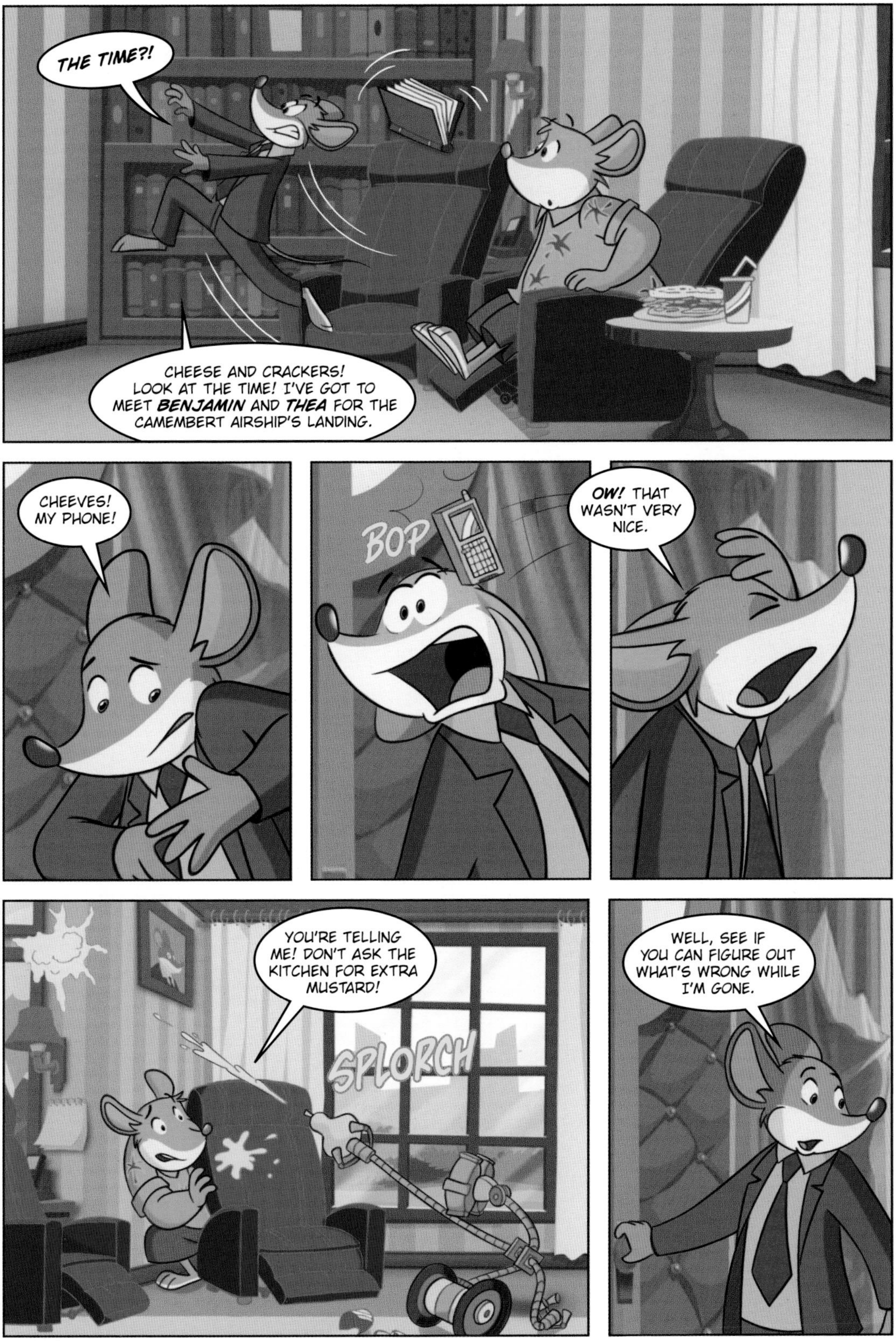
THE TIME?!
CHEESE AND CRACKERS! LOOK AT THE TIME! I'VE GOT TO MEET **BENJAMIN** AND **THEA** FOR THE CAMEMBERT AIRSHIP'S LANDING.
CHEEVES! MY PHONE!
BOP
OW! THAT WASN'T VERY NICE.
YOU'RE TELLING ME! DON'T ASK THE KITCHEN FOR EXTRA MUSTARD!
SPLORCH
WELL, SEE IF YOU CAN FIGURE OUT WHAT'S WRONG WHILE I'M GONE.

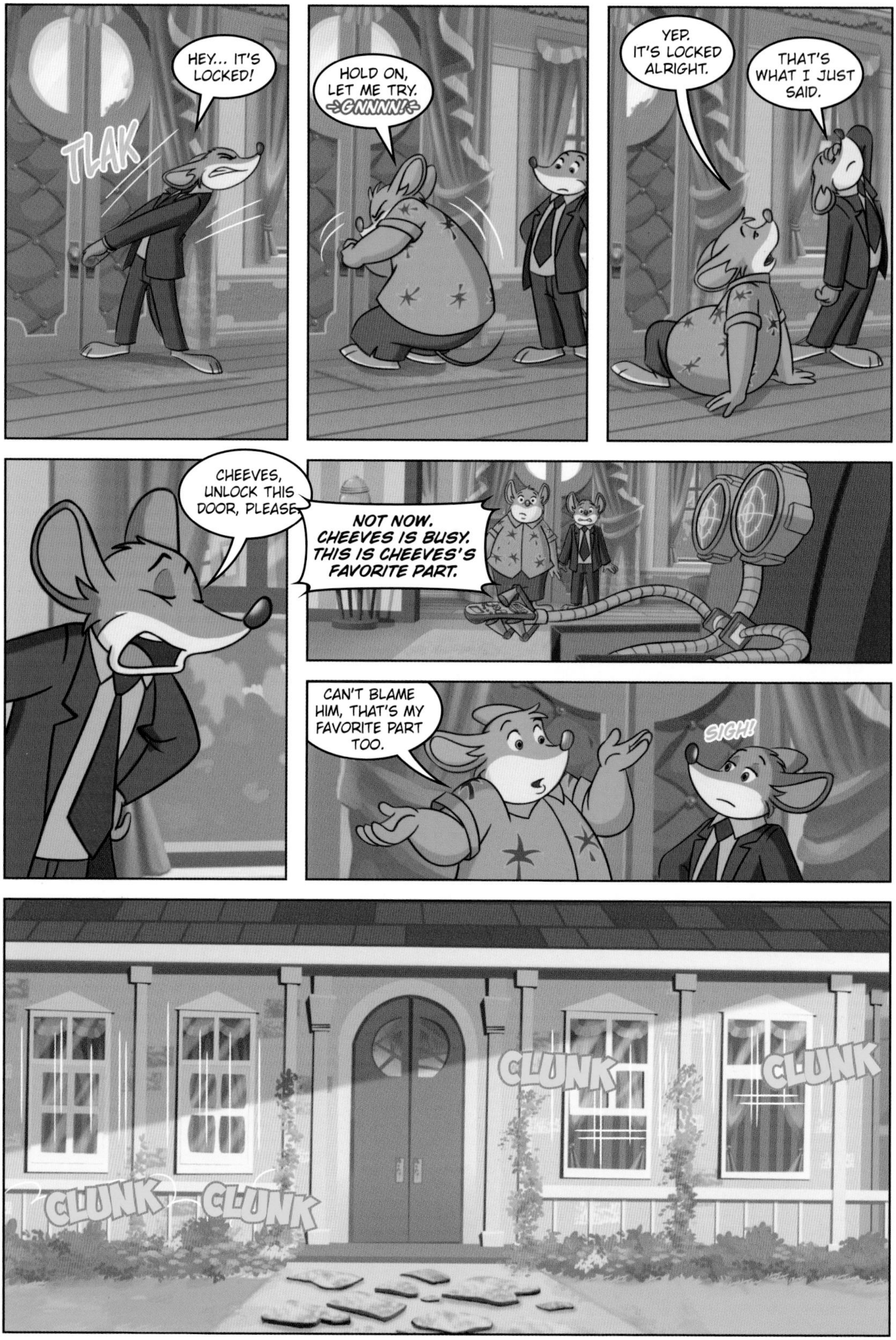
HEY... IT'S LOCKED!
TLAK
HOLD ON, LET ME TRY.
GNNNN!
YEP. IT'S LOCKED ALRIGHT.
THAT'S WHAT I JUST SAID.
CHEEVES, UNLOCK THIS DOOR, PLEASE.
NOT NOW. CHEEVES IS BUSY. THIS IS CHEEVES'S FAVORITE PART.
CAN'T BLAME HIM, THAT'S MY FAVORITE PART TOO.
SIGH!
CLUNK
CLUNK
CLUNK
CLUNK

-GNNNN!-

CHEEVES, IS THIS A PRANK?!

OOOH, LOOK! IT'S A BIG BALLOON-THING.

OH, NO! THE CAMEMBERT AIRSHIP! I'VE GOT TO GET OUT OF THE HOUSE, NOW!

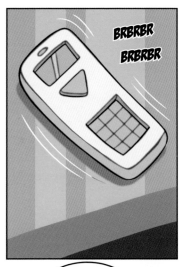

BRBRBR
BRBRBR

HELLO?

HELLO, PROFESSOR CHEESEWHEEL?! YOU NEED TO COME SHUT DOWN THIS HOUSE!

MMM-HM, STRANGE. IT DOES SOUND LIKE A SYSTEM ERROR. I'LL DROP BY IN A FEW HOURS.

I DON'T HAVE A FEW HOURS! THE CAMEMBERT AIRSHIP IS ARRIVING NOW!

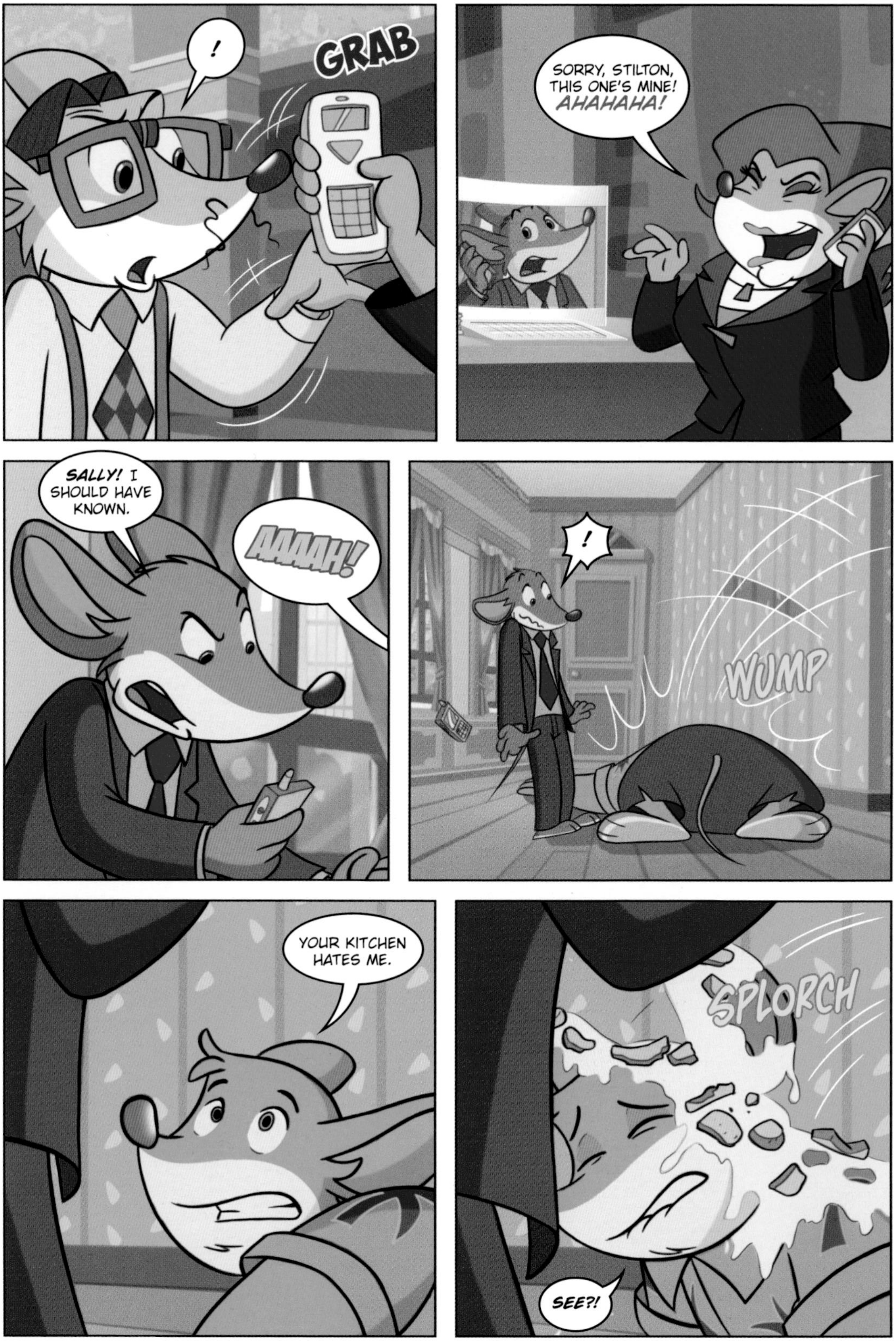
!
GRAB
SORRY, STILTON, THIS ONE'S MINE! AHAHAHA!
SALLY! I SHOULD HAVE KNOWN.
AAAAH!
!
WUMP
YOUR KITCHEN HATES ME.
SPLORCH
SEE?!

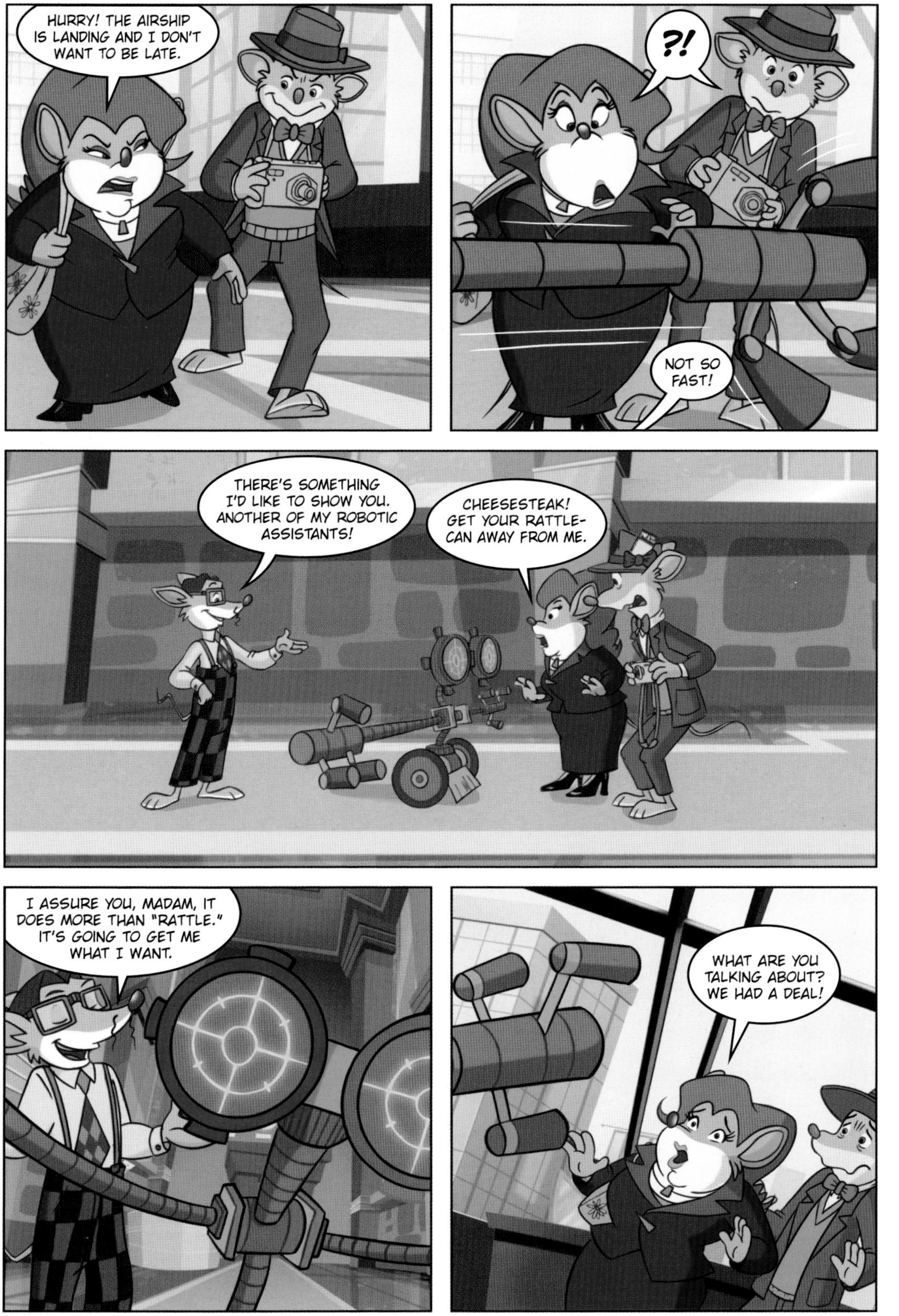
HURRY! THE AIRSHIP IS LANDING AND I DON'T WANT TO BE LATE.
?!
NOT SO FAST!
THERE'S SOMETHING I'D LIKE TO SHOW YOU. ANOTHER OF MY ROBOTIC ASSISTANTS!
CHEESESTEAK! GET YOUR RATTLE-CAN AWAY FROM ME.
I ASSURE YOU, MADAM, IT DOES MORE THAN "RATTLE." IT'S GOING TO GET ME WHAT I WANT.
WHAT ARE YOU TALKING ABOUT? WE HAD A DEAL!

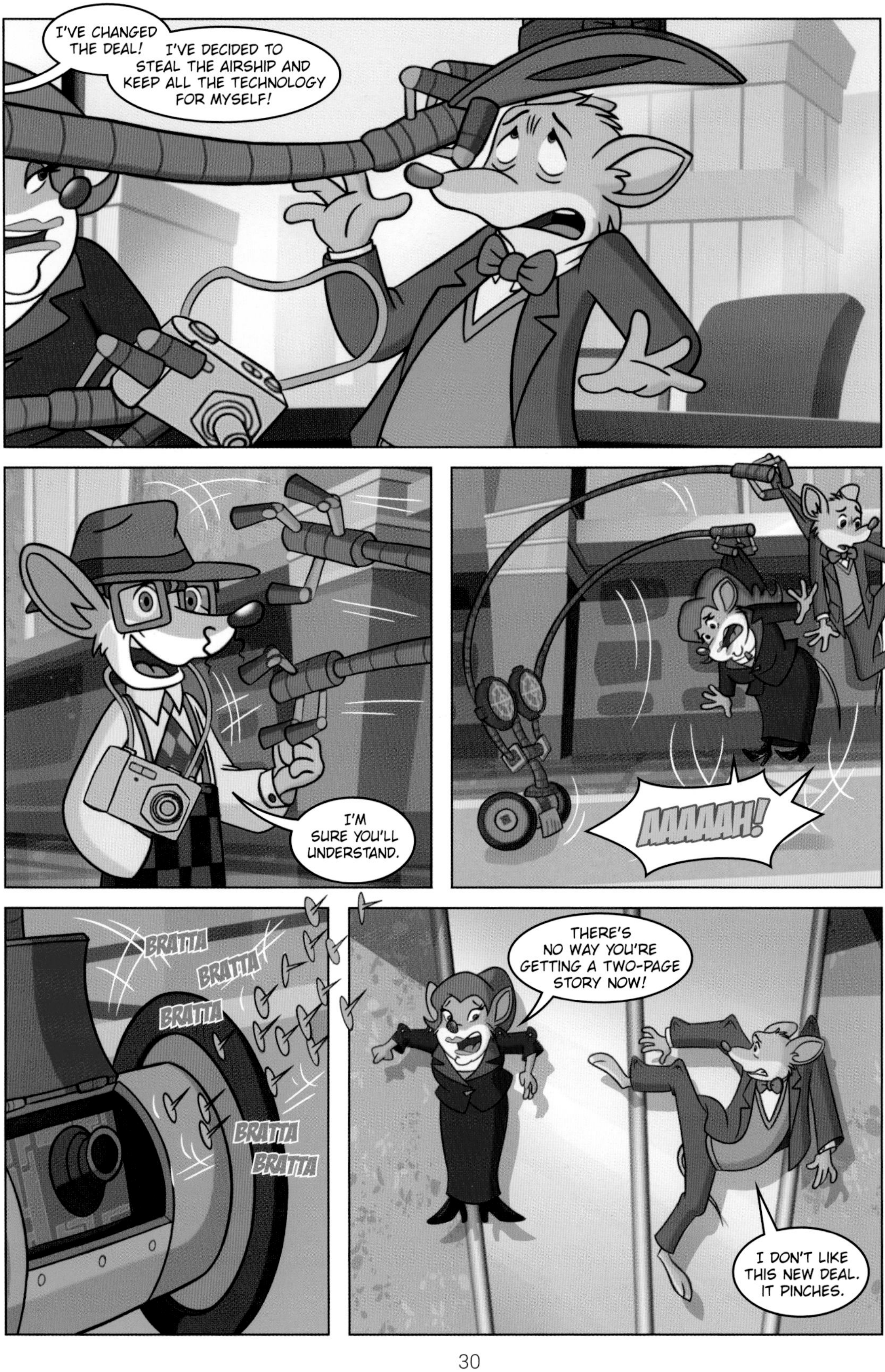
I'VE CHANGED THE DEAL!
I'VE DECIDED TO STEAL THE AIRSHIP AND KEEP ALL THE TECHNOLOGY FOR MYSELF!
I'M SURE YOU'LL UNDERSTAND.
AAAAAH!
BRATTA
BRATTA
BRATTA
BRATTA
BRATTA
THERE'S NO WAY YOU'RE GETTING A TWO-PAGE STORY NOW!
I DON'T LIKE THIS NEW DEAL. IT PINCHES.

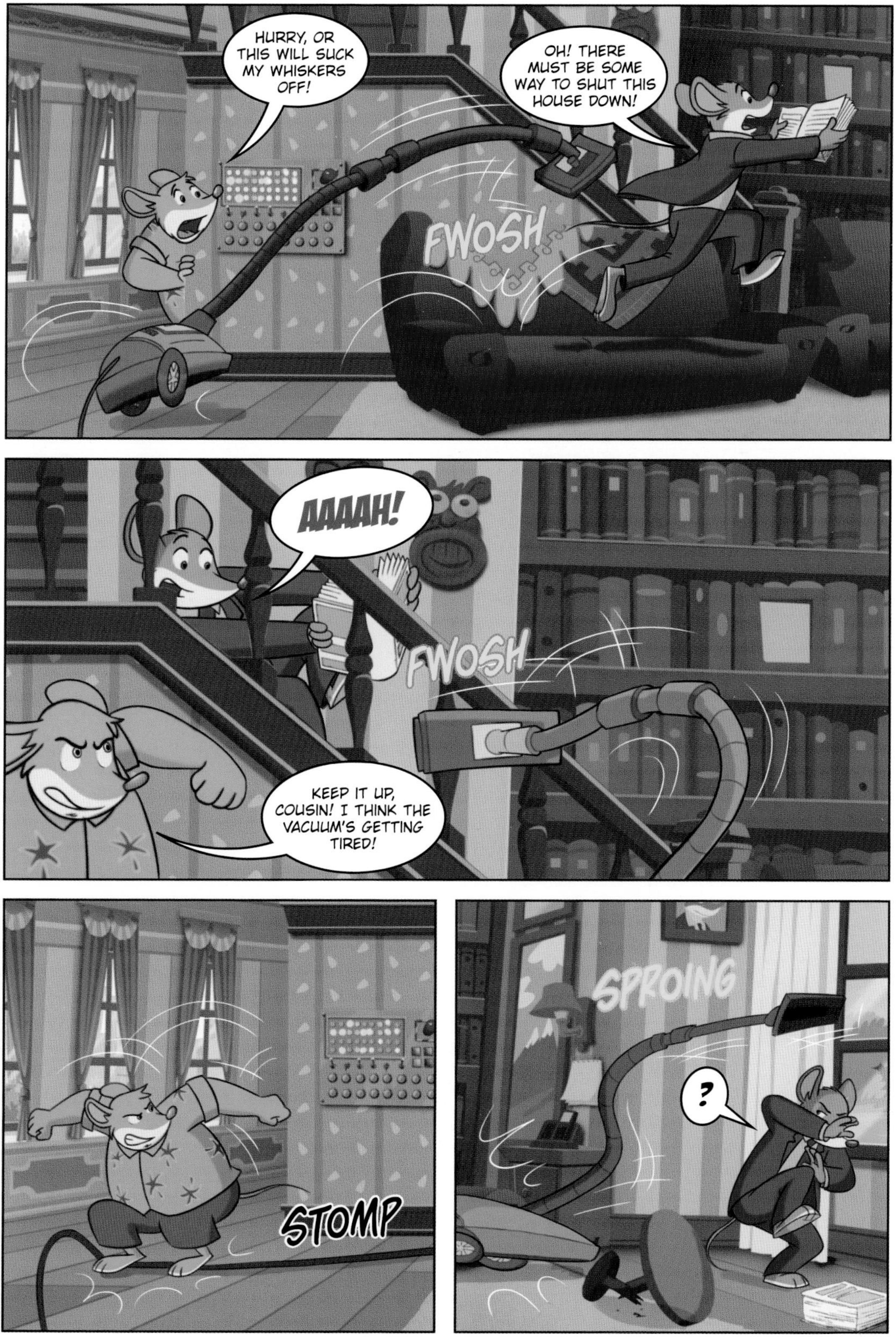
HURRY, OR THIS WILL SUCK MY WHISKERS OFF!
OH! THERE MUST BE SOME WAY TO SHUT THIS HOUSE DOWN!
FWOSH
AAAAH!
FWOSH
KEEP IT UP, COUSIN! I THINK THE VACUUM'S GETTING TIRED!
STOMP
SPROING
?

CRASH

FZZZZT

UH-OH!

CHEEVES! DO SOMETHING! THE HOUSE IS GOING NUTS!

PLEASE REFRAIN FROM LOUD OUTBURSTS. CHEEVES IS ENJOYING SOME QUALITY TIME.

ALERT!

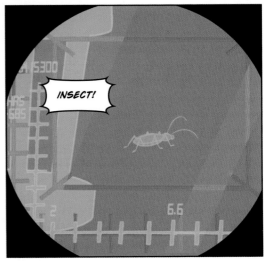

INSECT!

32

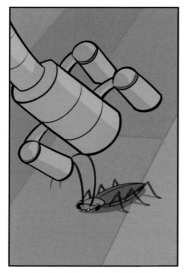

NOT ON MY CLEAN FLOOR!

NOW'S OUR CHANCE! *GO!*

GRRRR

FWOOOSH

! !

SUCK ON THIS!

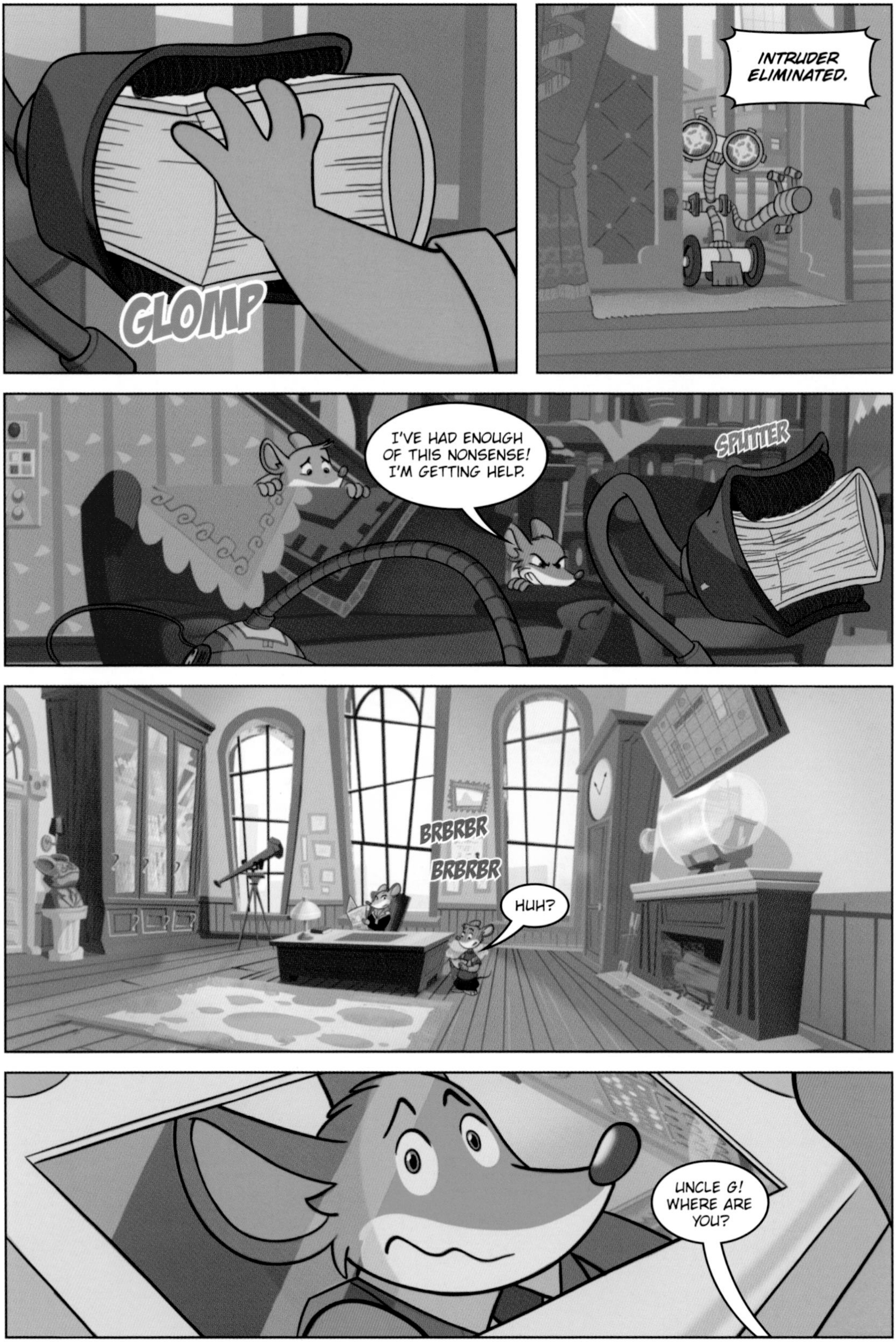
GLOMP
INTRUDER ELIMINATED.
I'VE HAD ENOUGH OF THIS NONSENSE! I'M GETTING HELP.
SPUTTER
BRBRBR
BRBRBR
HUH?
UNCLE G! WHERE ARE YOU?

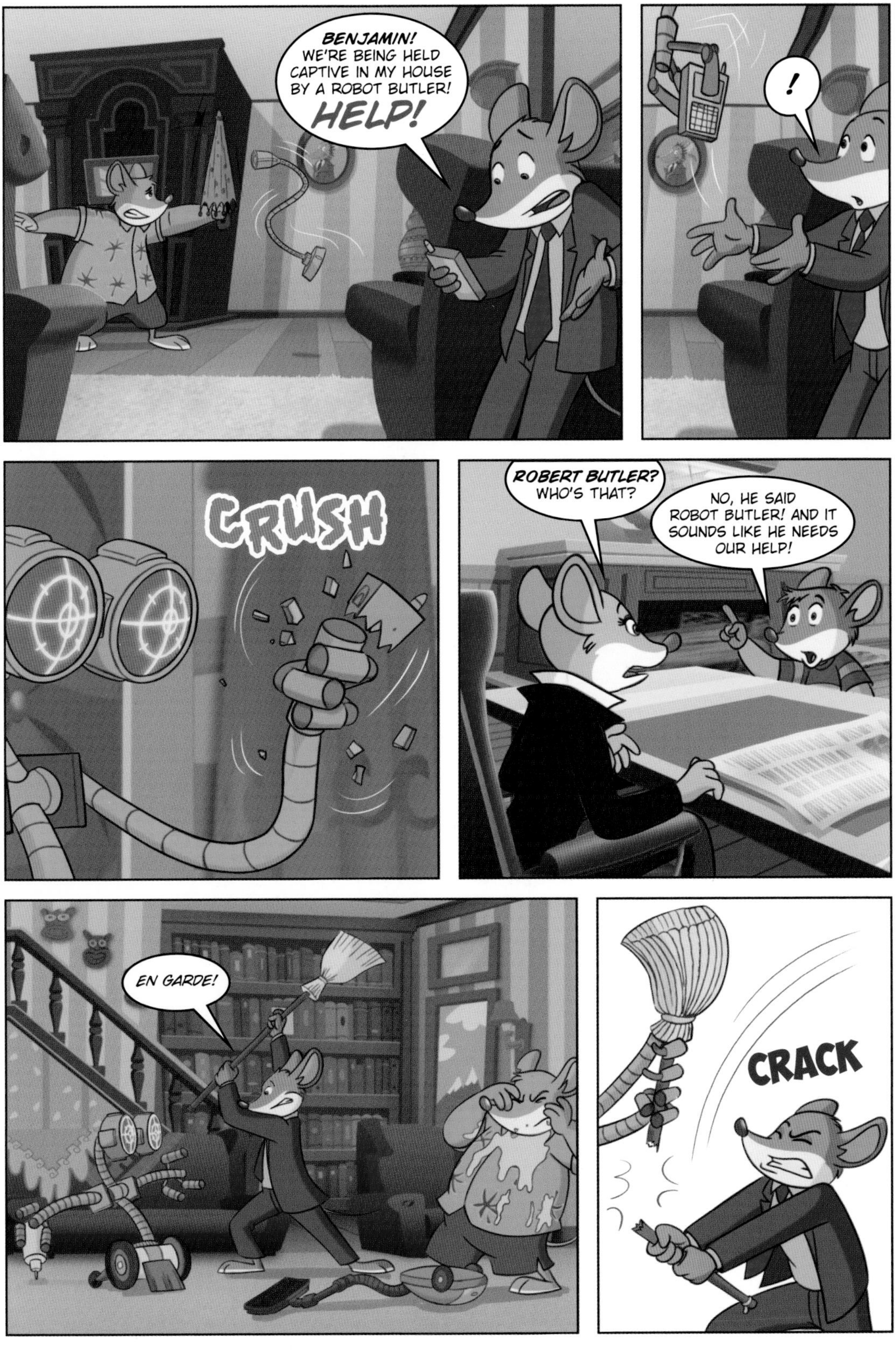

BENJAMIN! WE'RE BEING HELD CAPTIVE IN MY HOUSE BY A ROBOT BUTLER! HELP!
!
CRUSH
ROBERT BUTLER? WHO'S THAT?
NO, HE SAID ROBOT BUTLER! AND IT SOUNDS LIKE HE NEEDS OUR HELP!
EN GARDE!
CRACK

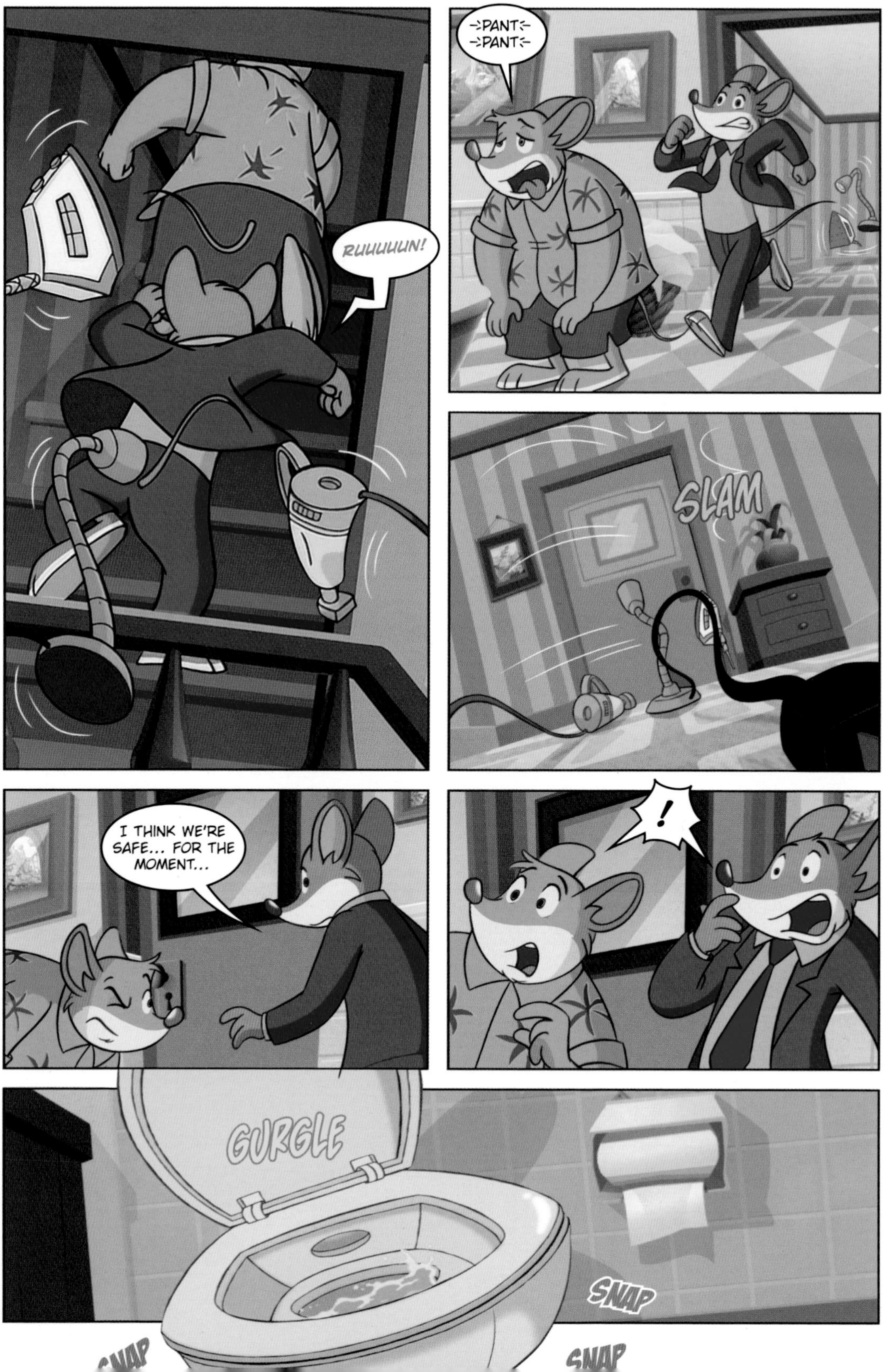
RUUUUUN!
PANT PANT
SLAM
I THINK WE'RE SAFE... FOR THE MOMENT...
!
GURGLE
SNAP
SNAP

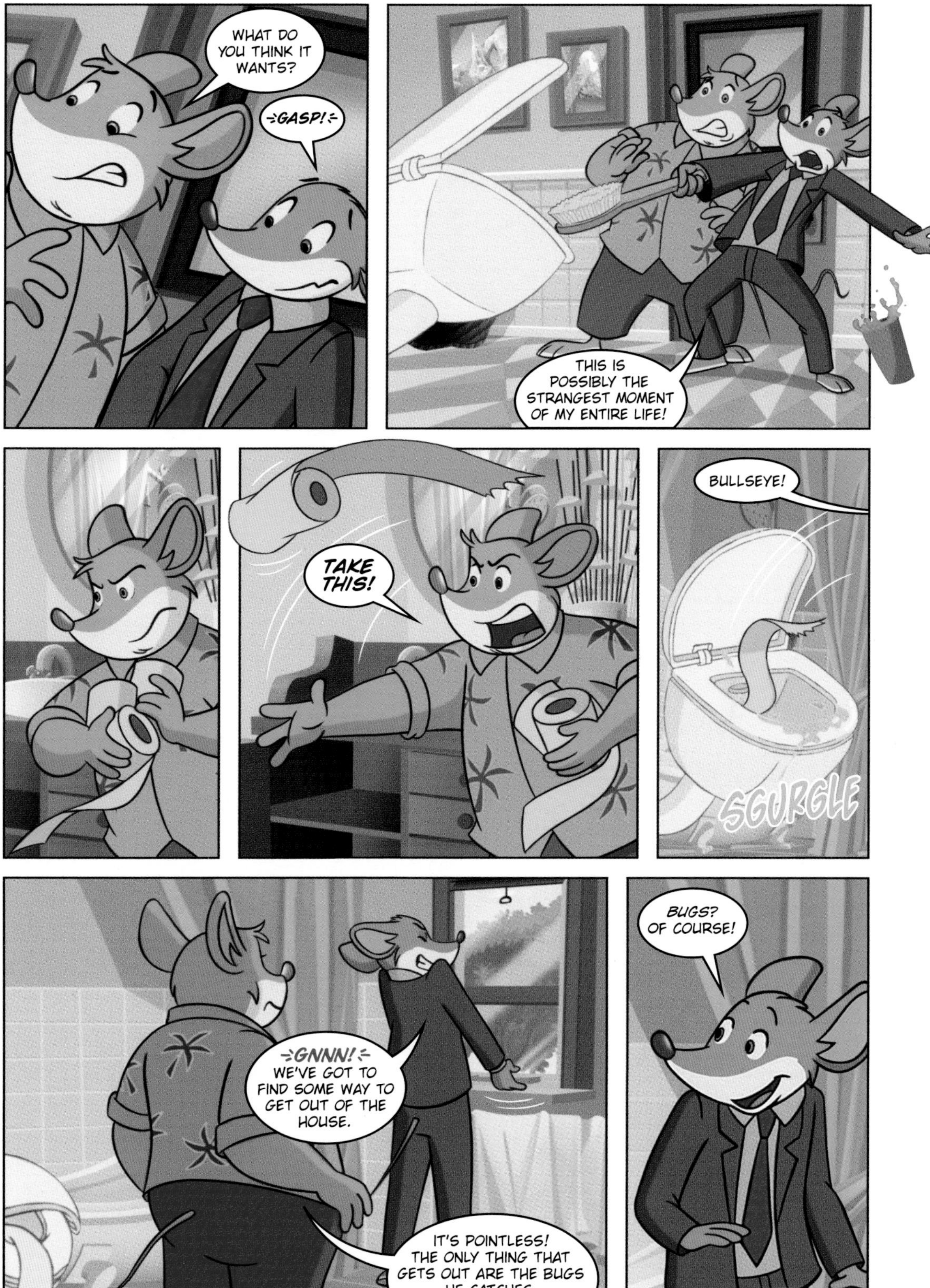
WHAT DO YOU THINK IT WANTS?
GASP!
THIS IS POSSIBLY THE STRANGEST MOMENT OF MY ENTIRE LIFE!
TAKE THIS!
BULLSEYE!
SGURGLE
GNNN! WE'VE GOT TO FIND SOME WAY TO GET OUT OF THE HOUSE.
IT'S POINTLESS! THE ONLY THING THAT GETS OUT ARE THE BUGS HE CATCHES.
BUGS? OF COURSE!

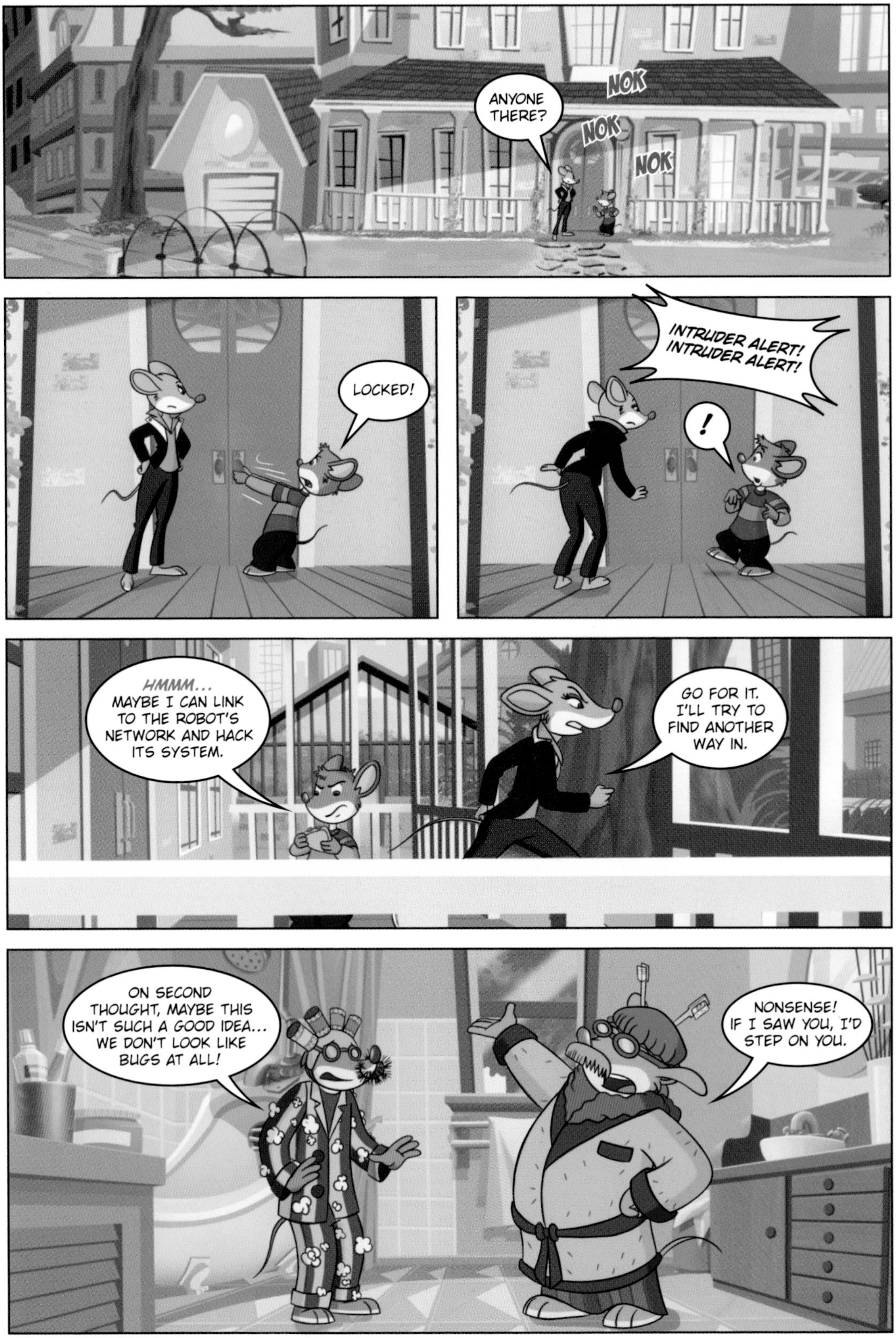
ANYONE THERE?
NOK
NOK
NOK
LOCKED!
INTRUDER ALERT! INTRUDER ALERT!
!
HMMM... MAYBE I CAN LINK TO THE ROBOT'S NETWORK AND HACK ITS SYSTEM.
GO FOR IT. I'LL TRY TO FIND ANOTHER WAY IN.
ON SECOND THOUGHT, MAYBE THIS ISN'T SUCH A GOOD IDEA... WE DON'T LOOK LIKE BUGS AT ALL!
NONSENSE! IF I SAW YOU, I'D STEP ON YOU.

I GUESS IT'S NOW OR NEVER.
IT'S BUG-TIME!
!
STOP IT! YOU'RE BENDING MY ANTENNAE!
INSECTS?!
FALSE ALARM: INSECT IMPOSTERS!
FZZZZT

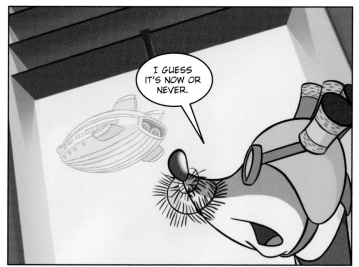

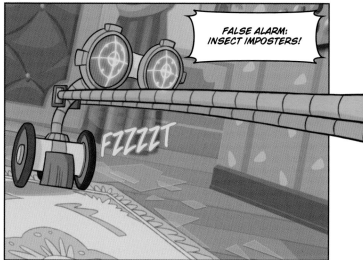

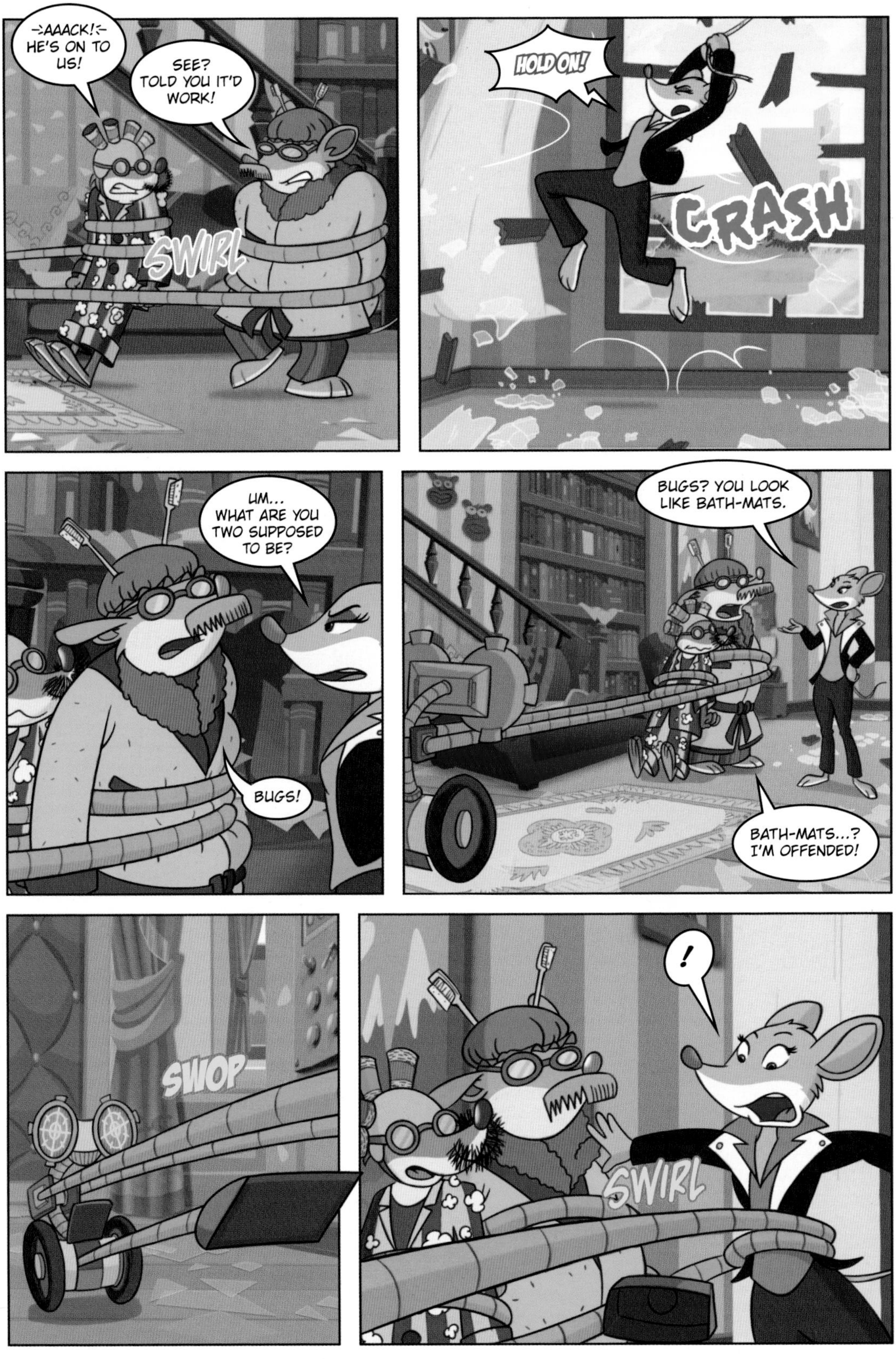
-AAACK!- HE'S ON TO US!
SEE? TOLD YOU IT'D WORK!
SWIRL
HOLD ON!
CRASH
UM... WHAT ARE YOU TWO SUPPOSED TO BE?
BUGS!
BUGS? YOU LOOK LIKE BATH-MATS.
BATH-MATS...? I'M OFFENDED!
SWOP
!
SWIRL

ALMOST THERE...

TAP
TAP
TAP

BLIP

HA! I'M IN! THIS'LL FIX YOUR SOFTWARE!

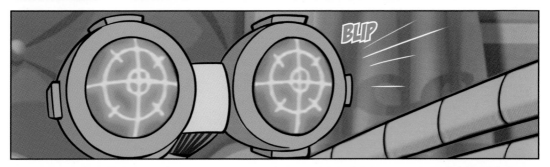

BLIP

?

TEA, MR. GERONIMO?

WHA... WHAT HAPPENED?

IT MUST HAVE BEEN BENJAMIN!

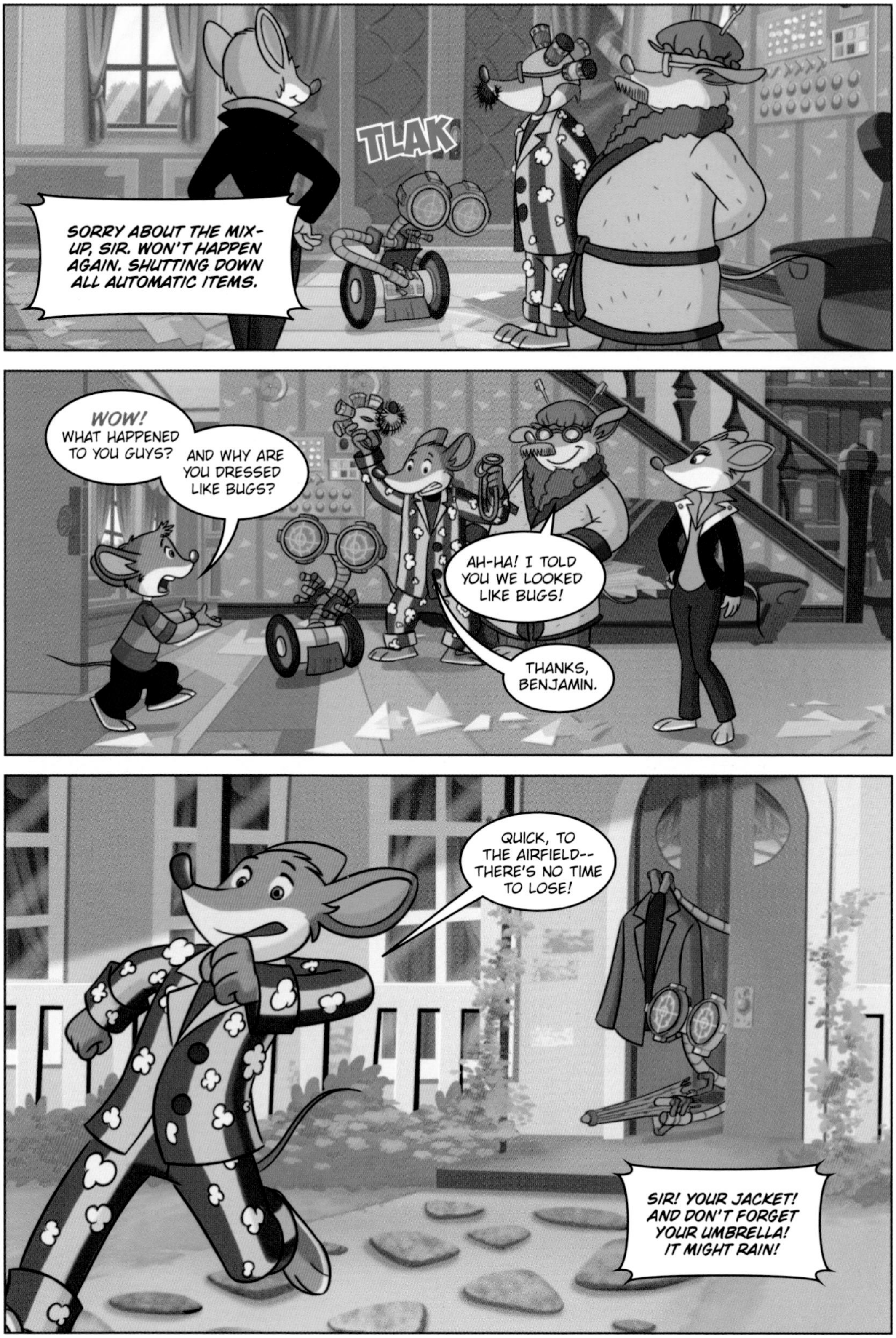
TLAK
SORRY ABOUT THE MIX-UP, SIR. WON'T HAPPEN AGAIN. SHUTTING DOWN ALL AUTOMATIC ITEMS.
WOW! WHAT HAPPENED TO YOU GUYS?
AND WHY ARE YOU DRESSED LIKE BUGS?
AH-HA! I TOLD YOU WE LOOKED LIKE BUGS!
THANKS, BENJAMIN.
QUICK, TO THE AIRFIELD-- THERE'S NO TIME TO LOSE!
SIR! YOUR JACKET! AND DON'T FORGET YOUR UMBRELLA! IT MIGHT RAIN!

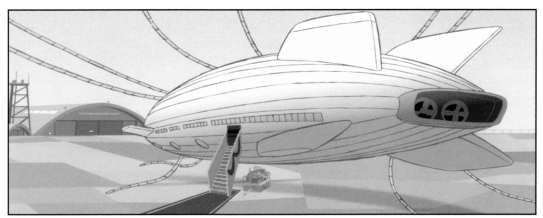

THE NAME IS... *SIMON SQUEELER*. I'M WITH THE... UM... THE DAILY RAT.

THE DAILY RAT, HUH?

I LOVE THE DAILY RAT! IS SALLY RATMOUSEN COMING, TOO?

SORRY, SHE'S ALL TIED UP.

STOP, IMPOSTER!

SKREEE

OH, NO! STILTON?!

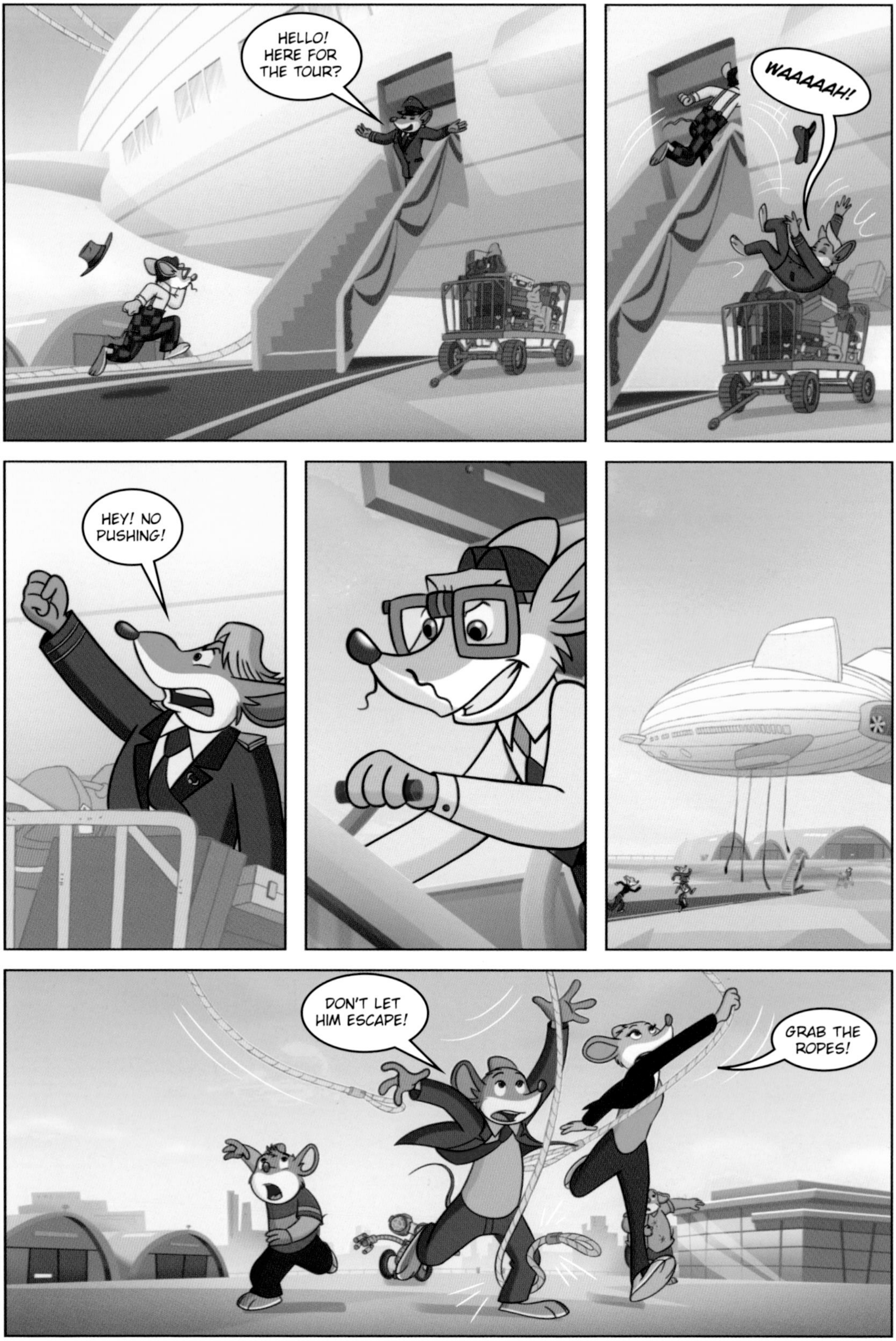
HELLO! HERE FOR THE TOUR?
WAAAAAH!
HEY! NO PUSHING!
DON'T LET HIM ESCAPE!
GRAB THE ROPES!

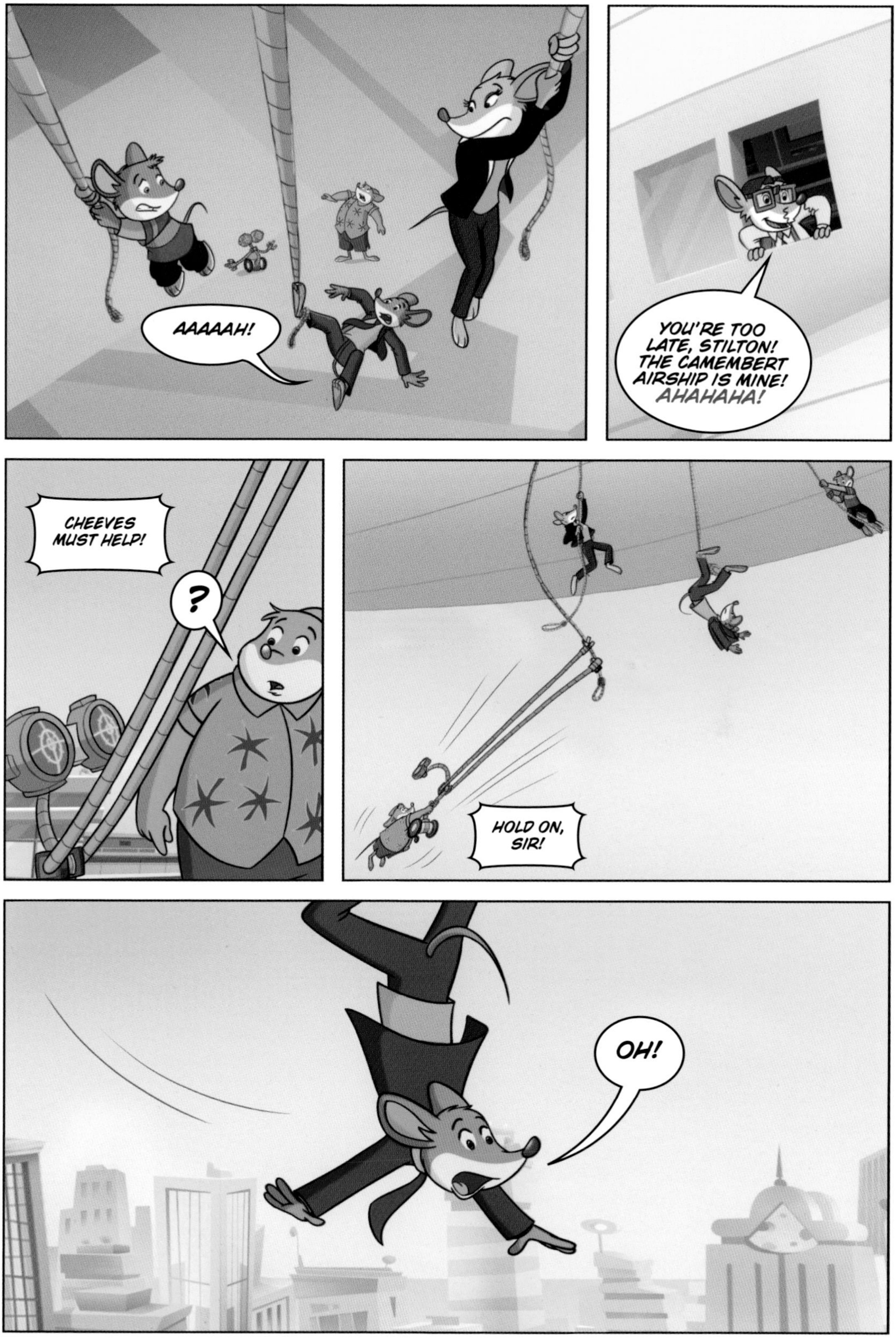
AAAAAH!
YOU'RE TOO LATE, STILTON! THE CAMEMBERT AIRSHIP IS MINE! AHAHAHA!
CHEEVES MUST HELP!
?
HOLD ON, SIR!
OH!

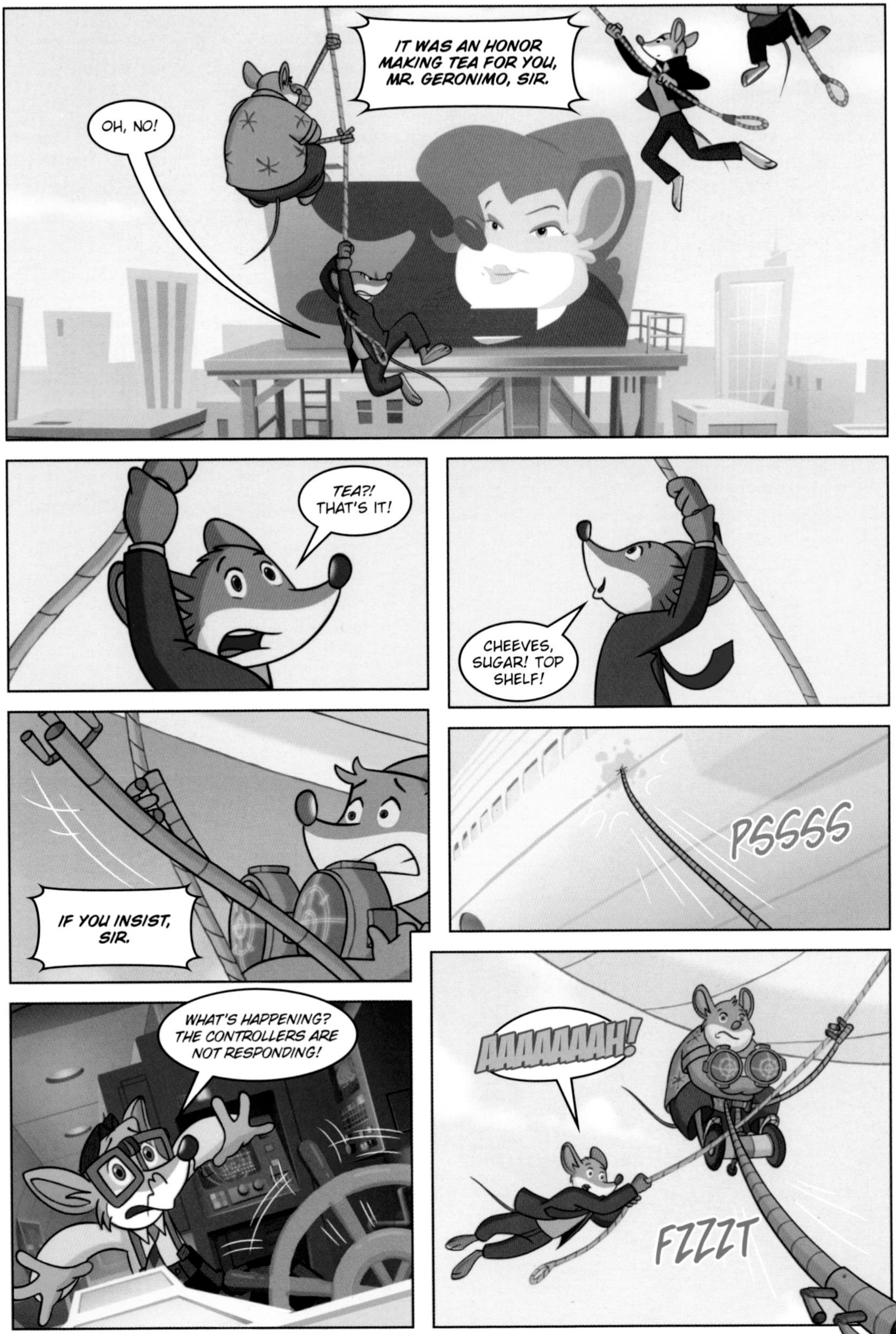
IT WAS AN HONOR MAKING TEA FOR YOU, MR. GERONIMO, SIR.
OH, NO!
TEA?! THAT'S IT!
CHEEVES, SUGAR! TOP SHELF!
IF YOU INSIST, SIR.
PSSSS
WHAT'S HAPPENING? THE CONTROLLERS ARE NOT RESPONDING!
AAAAAAAH!
FZZZT

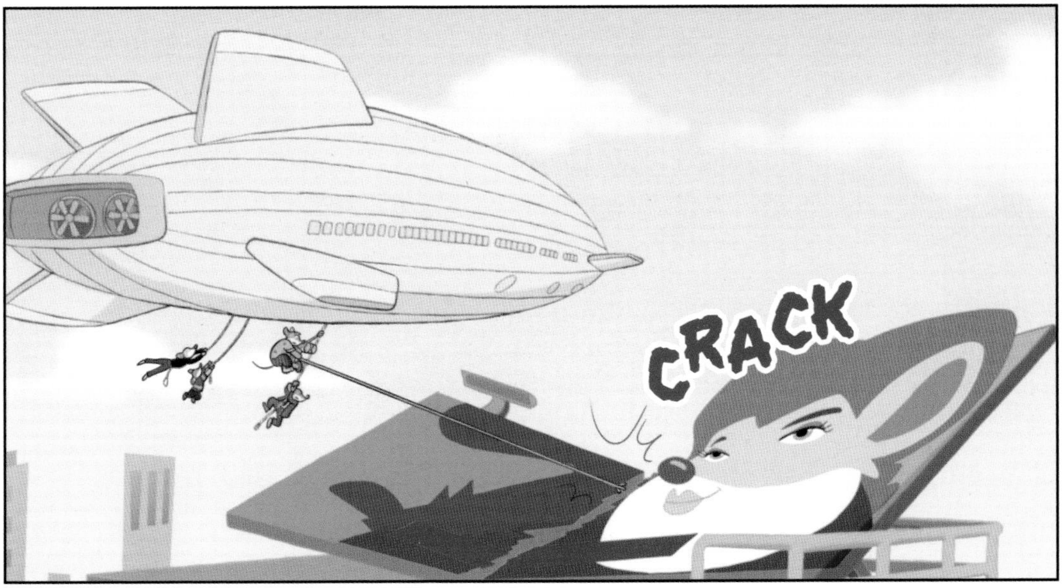
CRACK

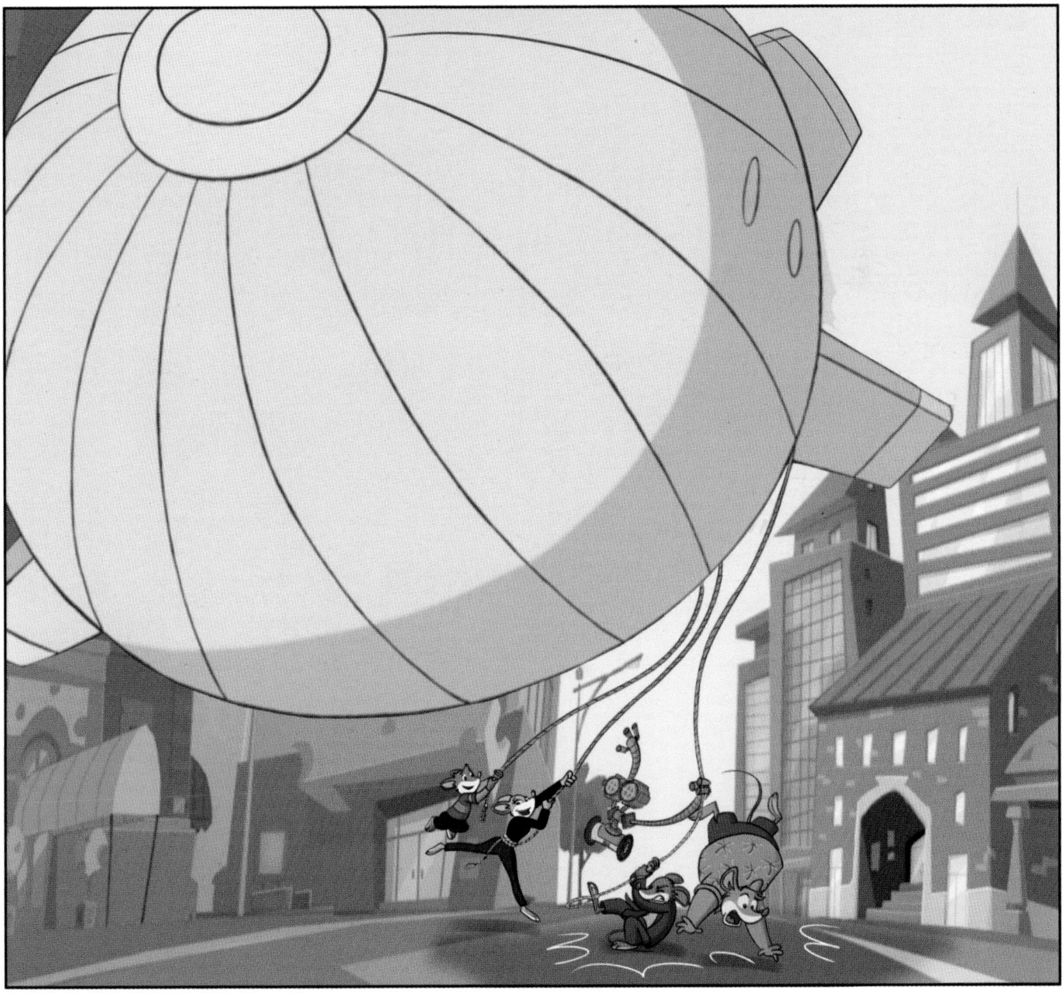

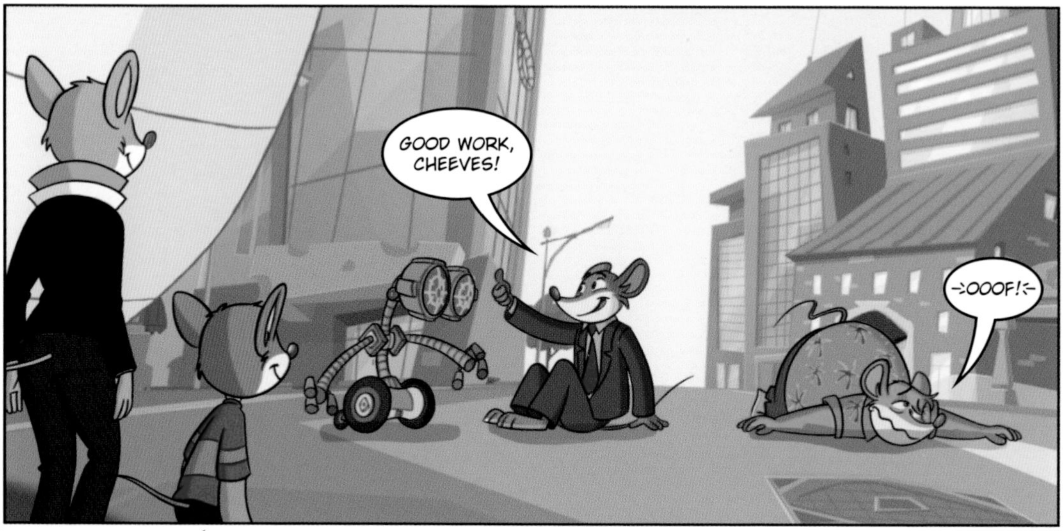
GOOD WORK, CHEEVES!
-OOOF!-

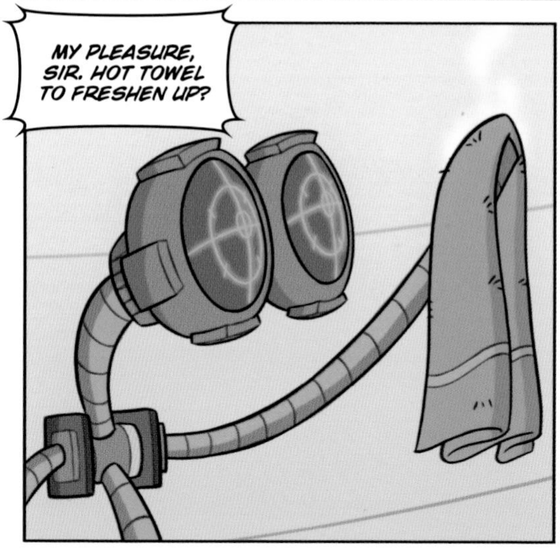
MY PLEASURE, SIR. HOT TOWEL TO FRESHEN UP?

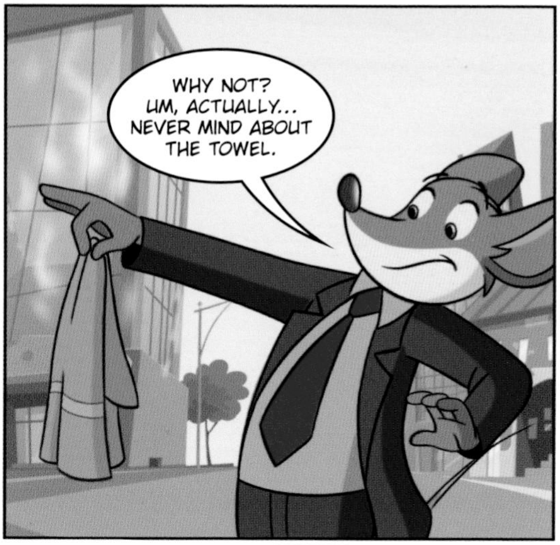
WHY NOT? UM, ACTUALLY... NEVER MIND ABOUT THE TOWEL.

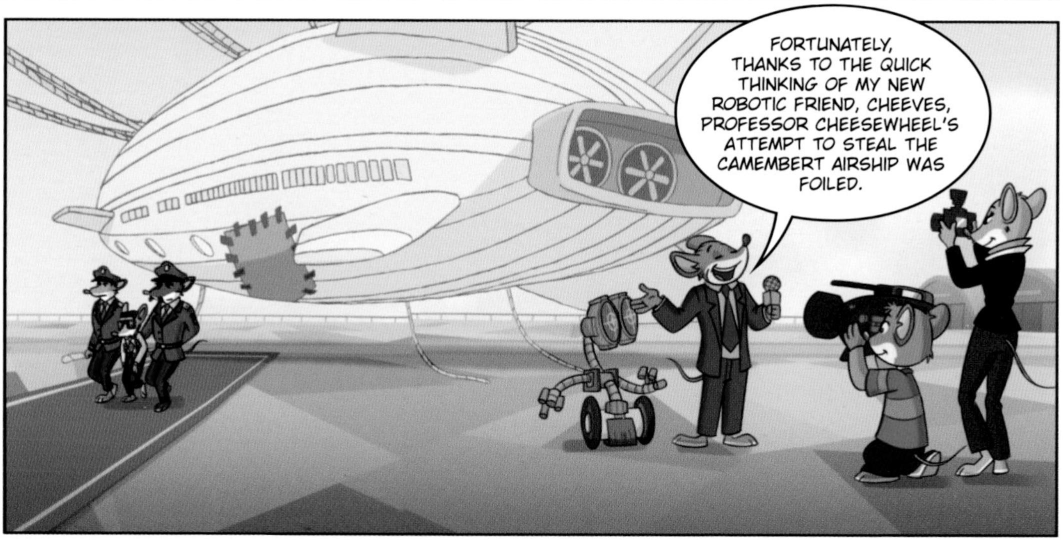
FORTUNATELY, THANKS TO THE QUICK THINKING OF MY NEW ROBOTIC FRIEND, CHEEVES, PROFESSOR CHEESEWHEEL'S ATTEMPT TO STEAL THE CAMEMBERT AIRSHIP WAS FOILED.

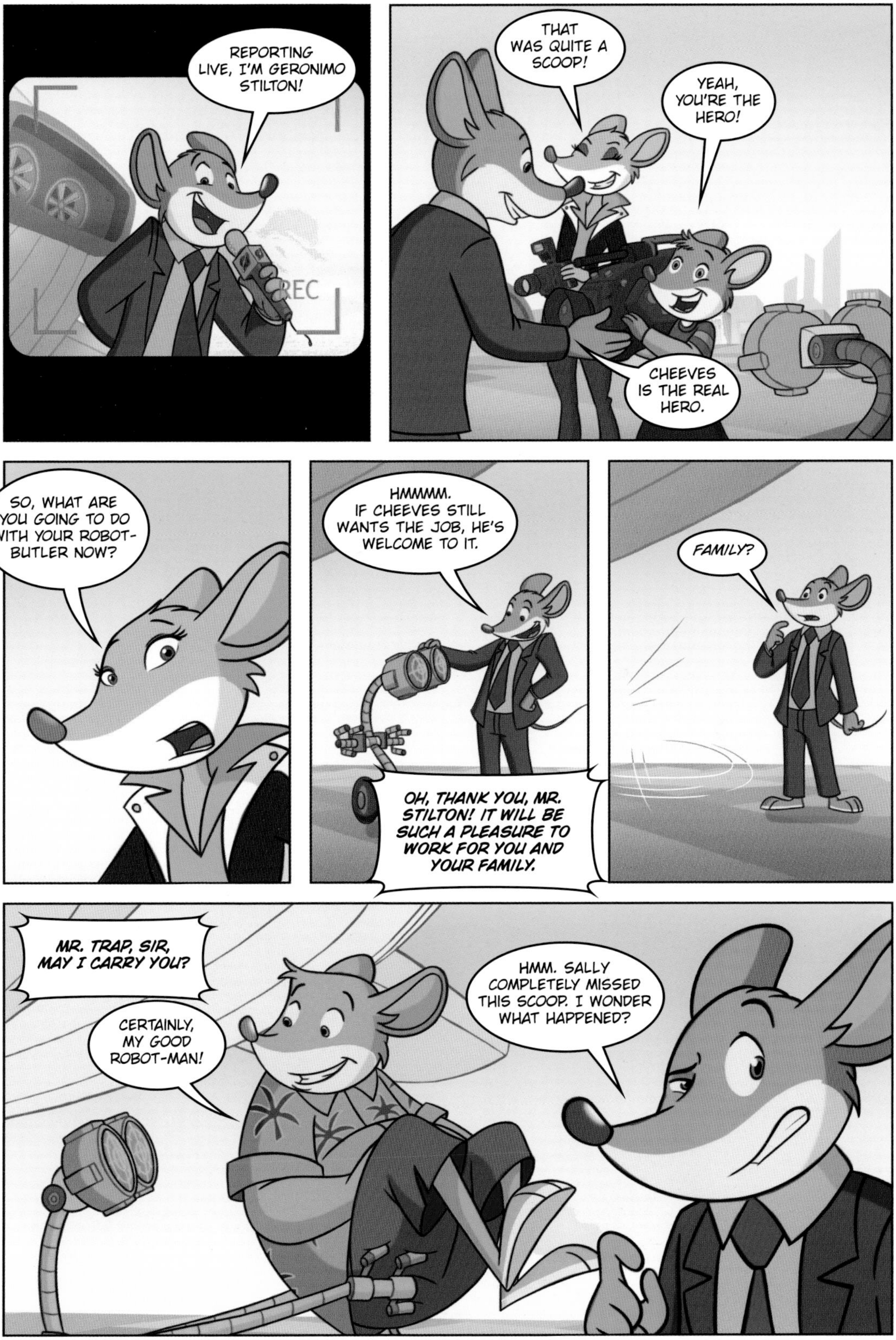
REPORTING LIVE, I'M GERONIMO STILTON!
REC
THAT WAS QUITE A SCOOP!
YEAH, YOU'RE THE HERO!
CHEEVES IS THE REAL HERO.
SO, WHAT ARE YOU GOING TO DO WITH YOUR ROBOT-BUTLER NOW?
HMMMM. IF CHEEVES STILL WANTS THE JOB, HE'S WELCOME TO IT.
OH, THANK YOU, MR. STILTON! IT WILL BE SUCH A PLEASURE TO WORK FOR YOU AND YOUR FAMILY.
FAMILY?
MR. TRAP, SIR, MAY I CARRY YOU?
CERTAINLY, MY GOOD ROBOT-MAN!
HMM. SALLY COMPLETELY MISSED THIS SCOOP. I WONDER WHAT HAPPENED?

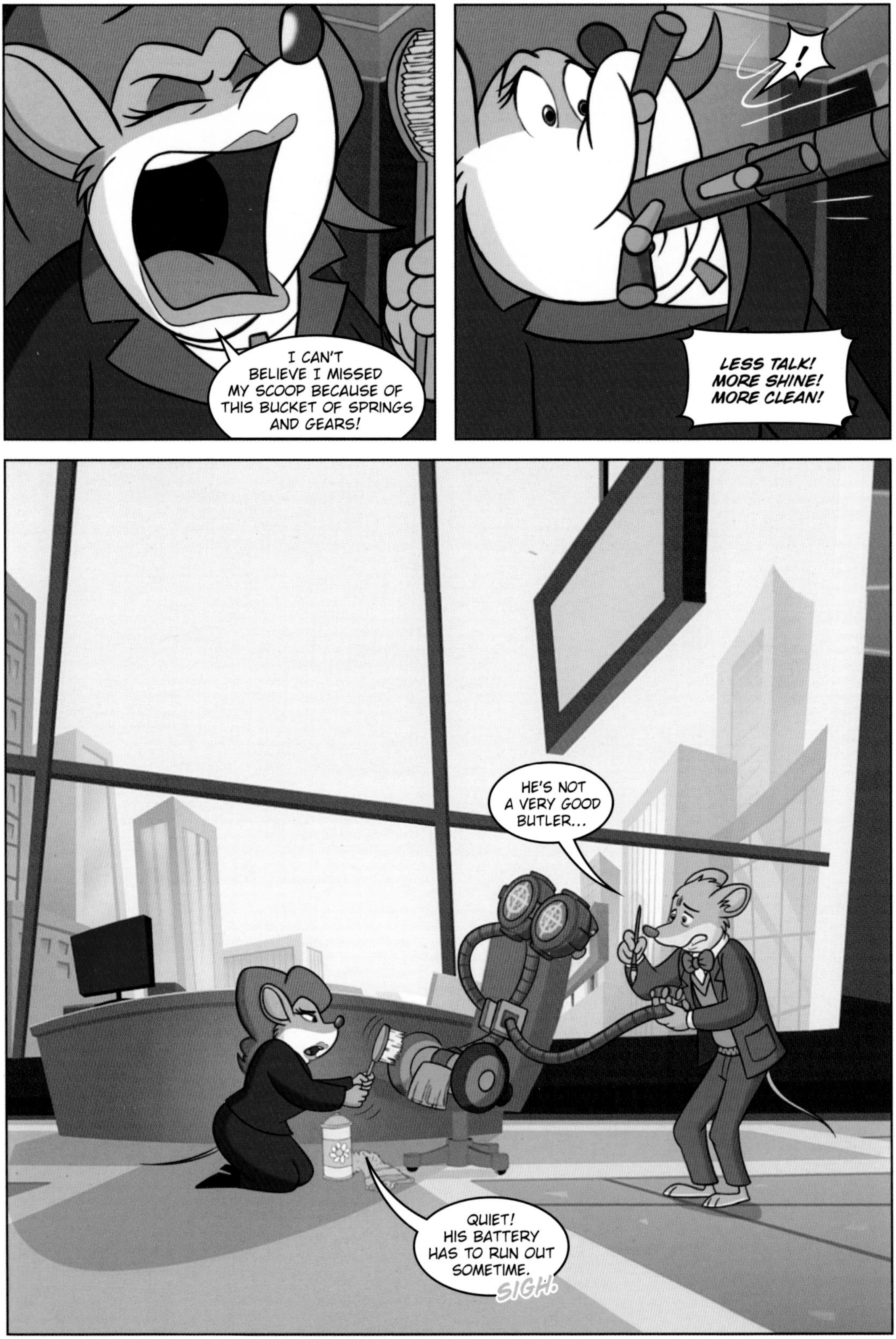
I CAN'T BELIEVE I MISSED MY SCOOP BECAUSE OF THIS BUCKET OF SPRINGS AND GEARS!
!
LESS TALK! MORE SHINE! MORE CLEAN!
HE'S NOT A VERY GOOD BUTLER...
QUIET! HIS BATTERY HAS TO RUN OUT SOMETIME.
SIGH.

Watch Out For PAPERCUTZ™

Welcome to the timeless twelfth GERONIMO STILTON REPORTER graphic novel, "The Mouse House of the Future," the official comics adaptation of *Geronimo Stilton*, animated series, Season One, episode twelve, written by Tom Mason and Dan Danko, brought to you by Papercutz—those office squatters dedicated to publishing great graphic novels for all ages. I'm Salicrup, *Jim Salicrup*, the Editor-in-Chief and Professional Cheese-Cutter, here to expound and pontificate about "The Rule of Three."

Actually, and not really surprising, there are more than one Rule of Three. There's a Rule of Three that relates directly to comedy writing. Basically, it's creating a joke that's also called a "triple." The way it works is listing a few things, where a pattern is created by the first two things listed, and the third thing listed winds up breaking that pattern to comic effect. For example, if I listed the three most important meals of the day as breakfast, lunch, and snack time. Snack time, while certainly enjoyable, isn't necessarily an especially healthy or important meal, thus being included as such is a little surprising and therefore funny.

Other Rules of Three may refer to a grouping of three words, or three paragraphs, or even 3 graphic novels...

The Three Bears, The Three Stooges, Three Blind Mice.

See no evil, hear no evil, speak no evil.

In the world of breakfast cereals there's even Snap, Crackle, and Pop.

Fans of ASTERIX (as well as Obelix, and Dogmatix), have probably seen our footnotes translating the Latin phrase, "Veni, vidi, vici," most often spoken by Julius Caesar, as "I came, I saw, I conquered." Well, not entirely, but that's another story.

Even in the Declaration of Independence of the United States, you'll find our Rights include, "Life, Liberty, and the Pursuit of Happiness."

And one of our favorite ways to pursue Happiness at Papercutz is to enjoy graphic novels, which brings us to the various 3 IN 1 series that we proudly publish. While the previously mentioned ASTERIX graphic novel series isn't called ASTERIX 3 IN 1, it may as well be, as each volume collects three classic ASTERIX graphic novels, that Papercutz hadn't published individually. Likewise THE SMURFS TALES features three graphic novels by Smurfs-creator Peyo that hadn't been published by Papercutz before (with an exception or two), while THE SMURFS 3 IN 1 collects previously published Papercutz graphic novels of THE SMURFS.

While there hasn't been a GERONIMO STILON REPORTER 3 IN 1 series yet, there is, however, a GERONIMO STILTON 3 IN 1 series that collects Geronimo's time-traveling graphic novels, in which he would strive to save the future, by protecting the past from the Pirate Cats—which there were three, Catardone III, Tersilla, and Bonzo.

The latest and greatest 3 IN 1 series are THE CASAGRANDES 3 IN 1 #1, which collects the first three graphic novels of THE CASAGRANDES and THE SISTERS 3 IN 1 #1 which, you may have already guessed, collects the first three graphic novels of THE SISTERS.

Also not surprisingly, variations of this very WATCH OUT FOR PAPERCUTZ column is appearing in three different graphic novels: LOUD HOUSE #17, THE SISTERS #8, and GERONIMO STILTON REPORTER #12. Hey, you wouldn't me to break the Rule of Three, would you?

(Oh, and don't miss the preview of GERONIMO STILTON REPORTER #13 "Reported Missing," starting on the next page!)

Thanks,

Jim

STAY IN TOUCH!

EMAIL:	salicrup@papercutz.com
WEB:	papercutz.com
TWITTER:	@papercutzgn
INSTAGRAM:	@papercutzgn
FACEBOOK:	PAPERCUTZGRAPHICNOVELS
SNAIL MAIL:	Papercutz, 160 Broadway, Suite 700, East Wing, New York, NY 10038

Go to papercutz.com and sign up for the free Papercutz e-newsletter!

Special Preview of GERONIMO STILTON REPORTER Graphic Novel #13 "Reported Missing"!

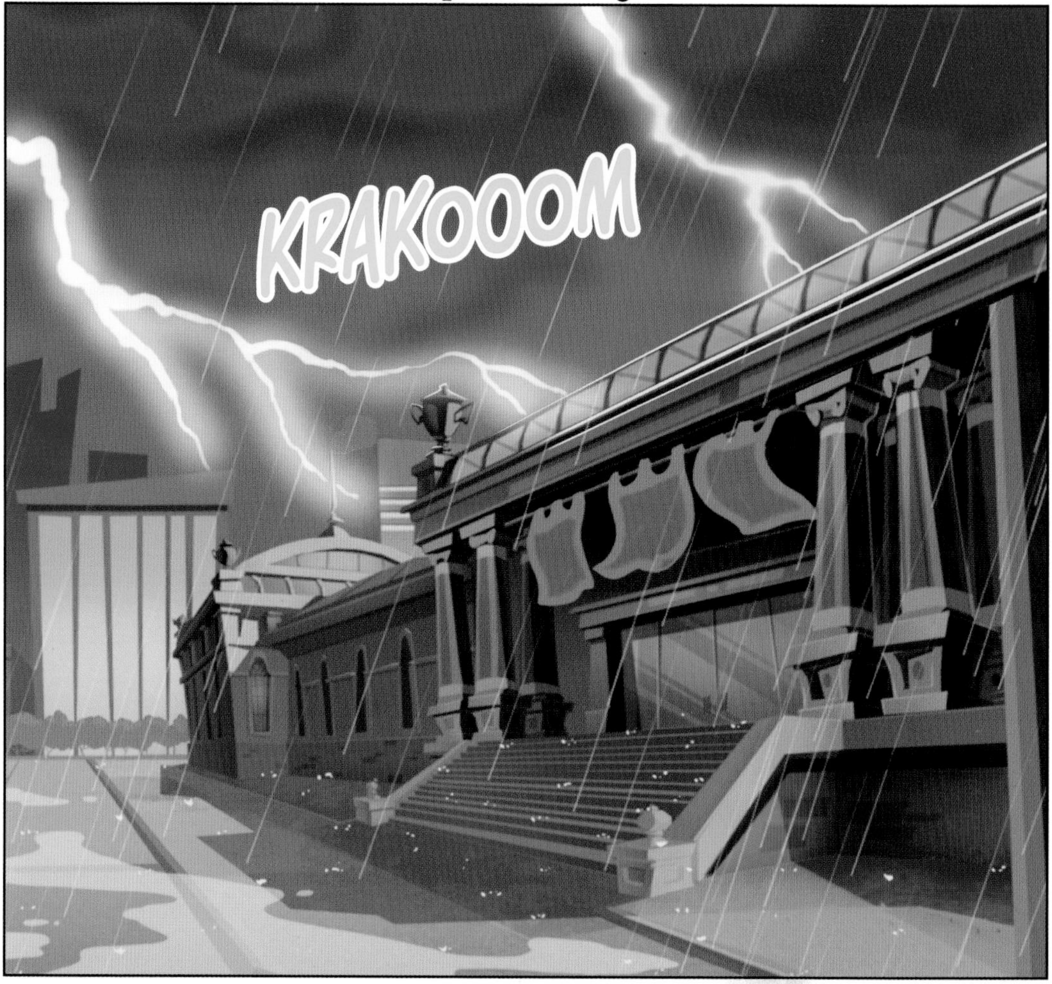
KRAKOOOM

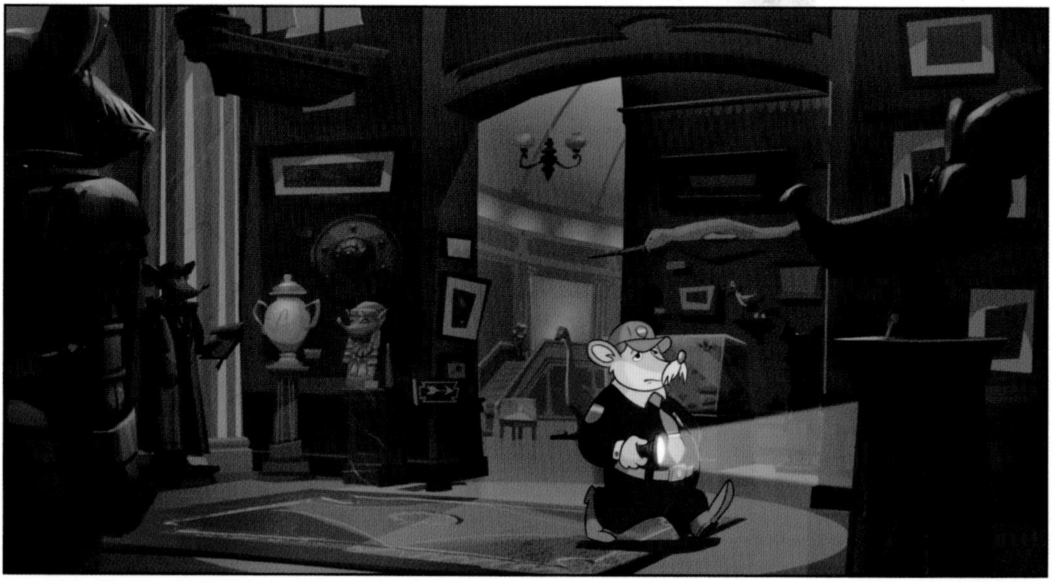

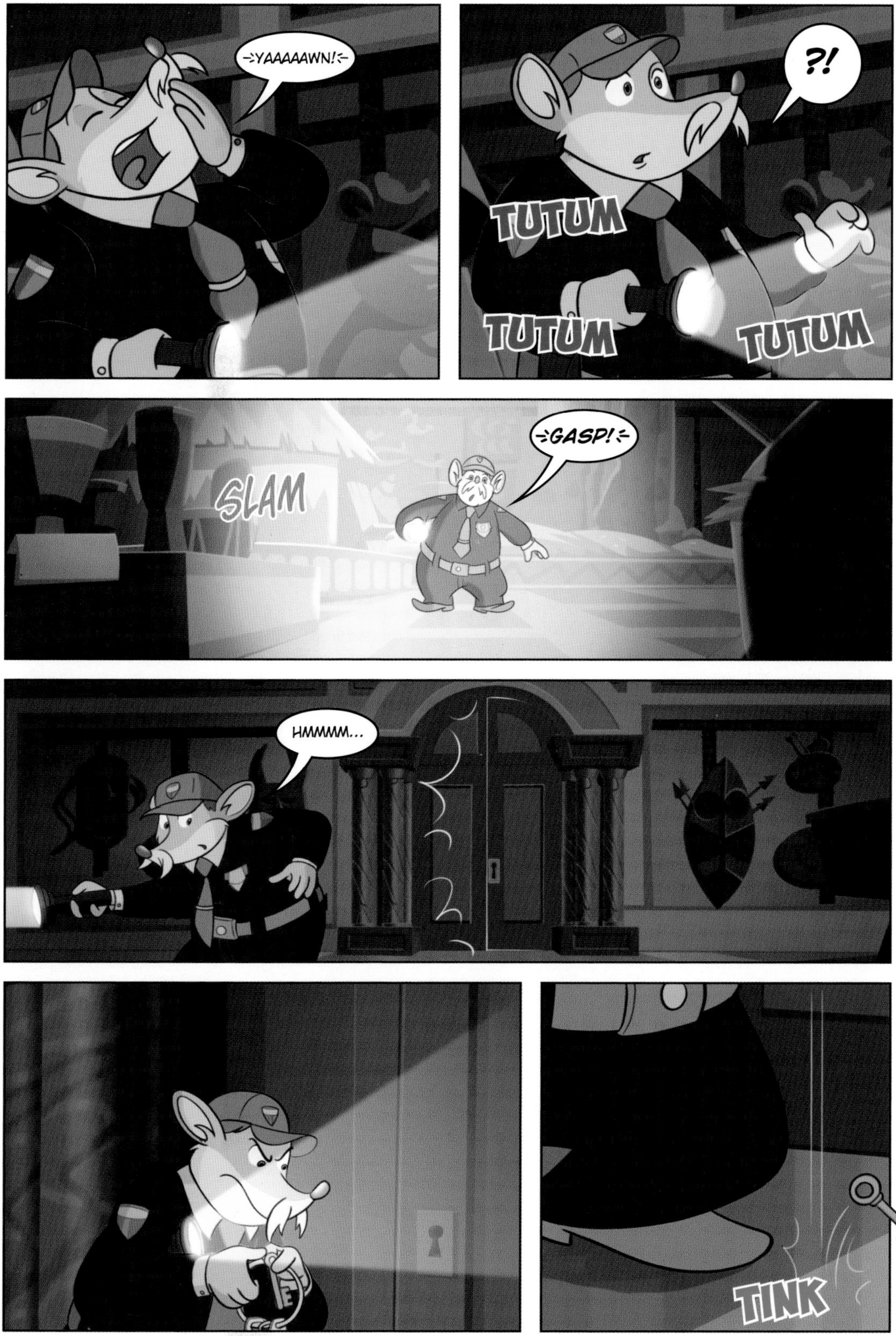
YAAAAAWN!
?!
TUTUM
TUTUM
TUTUM
SLAM
GASP!
HMMMM...
TINK

STHNC

WHO'S THERE--?!

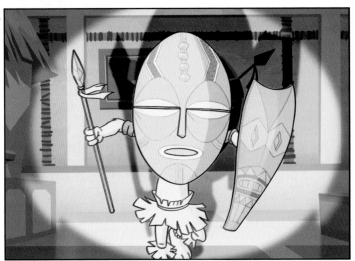

AAAAAAH!

EXTRA, EXTRA! MUSEUM TERRORIZED BY *AFRICAN SPIRITS!* NIGHT WATCHMAN FROZEN IN FEAR!

DAILY RAT

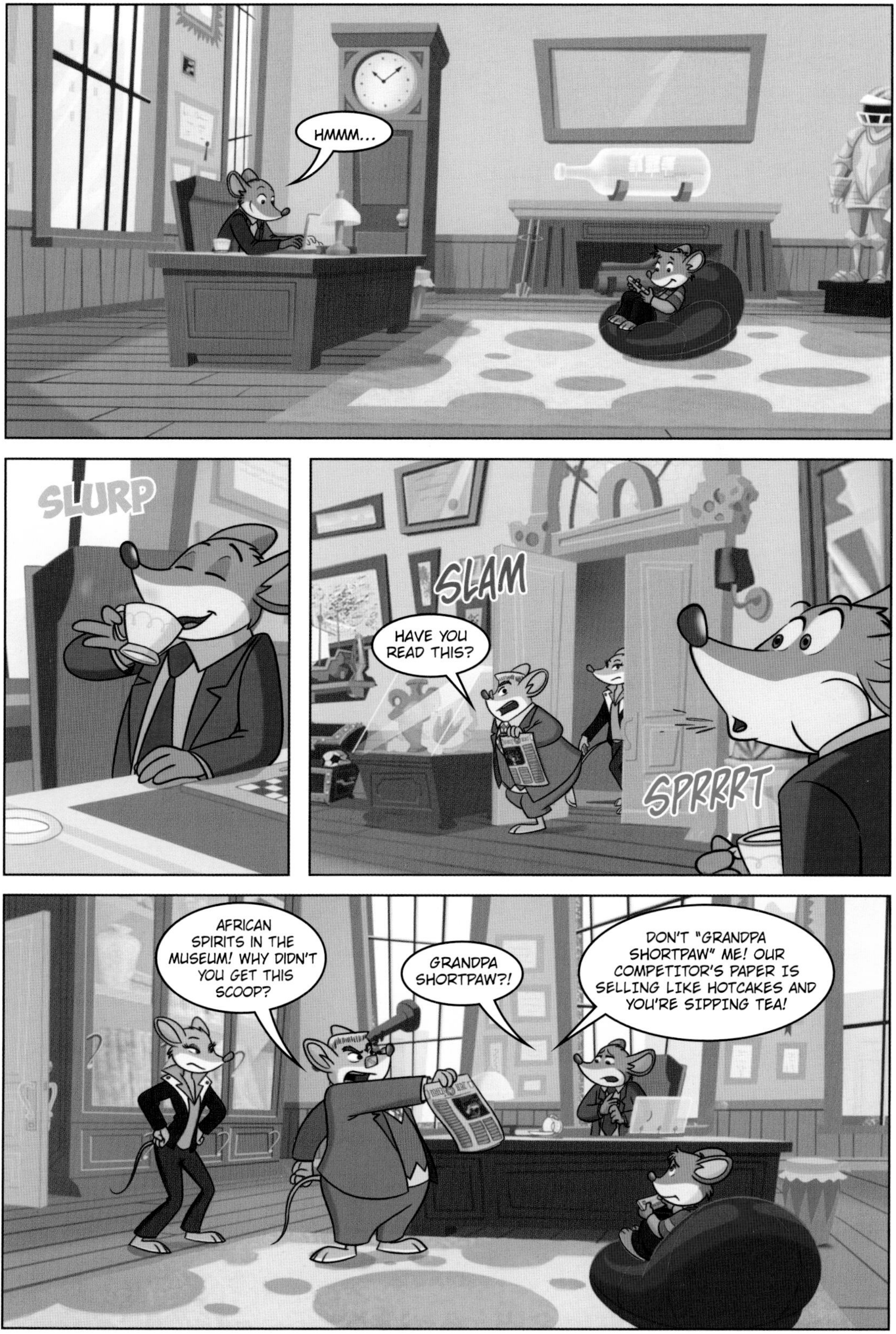
HMMM...
SLURP
SLAM
HAVE YOU READ THIS?
SPRRRT
AFRICAN SPIRITS IN THE MUSEUM! WHY DIDN'T YOU GET THIS SCOOP?
GRANDPA SHORTPAW?!
DON'T "GRANDPA SHORTPAW" ME! OUR COMPETITOR'S PAPER IS SELLING LIKE HOTCAKES AND YOU'RE SIPPING TEA!

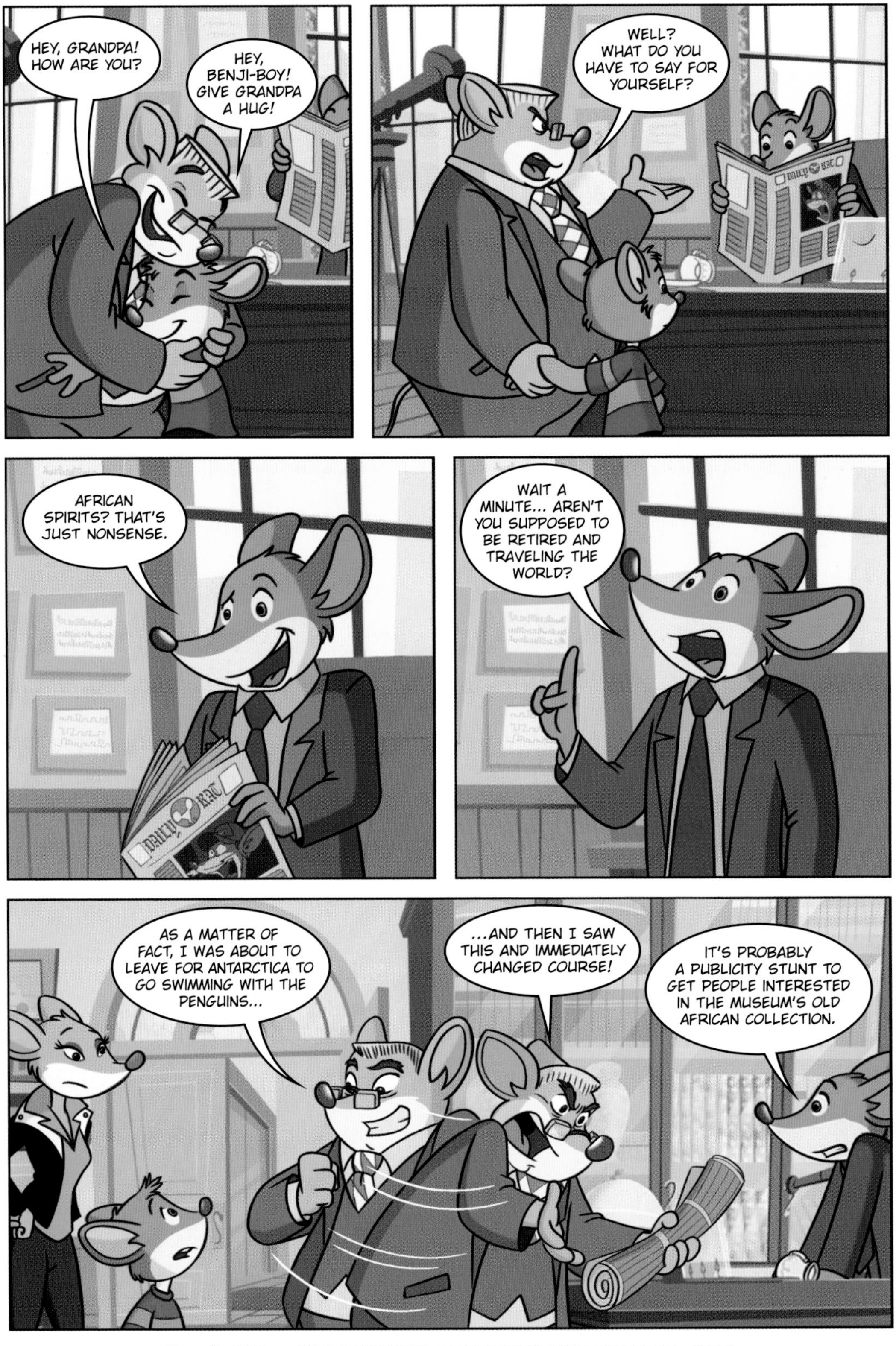
HEY, GRANDPA! HOW ARE YOU?
HEY, BENJI-BOY! GIVE GRANDPA A HUG!
WELL? WHAT DO YOU HAVE TO SAY FOR YOURSELF?
AFRICAN SPIRITS? THAT'S JUST NONSENSE.
WAIT A MINUTE... AREN'T YOU SUPPOSED TO BE RETIRED AND TRAVELING THE WORLD?
AS A MATTER OF FACT, I WAS ABOUT TO LEAVE FOR ANTARCTICA TO GO SWIMMING WITH THE PENGUINS...
...AND THEN I SAW THIS AND IMMEDIATELY CHANGED COURSE!
IT'S PROBABLY A PUBLICITY STUNT TO GET PEOPLE INTERESTED IN THE MUSEUM'S OLD AFRICAN COLLECTION.

Don't Miss GERONIMO STILTON REPORTER #13 "Reported Missing"! Coming soon!

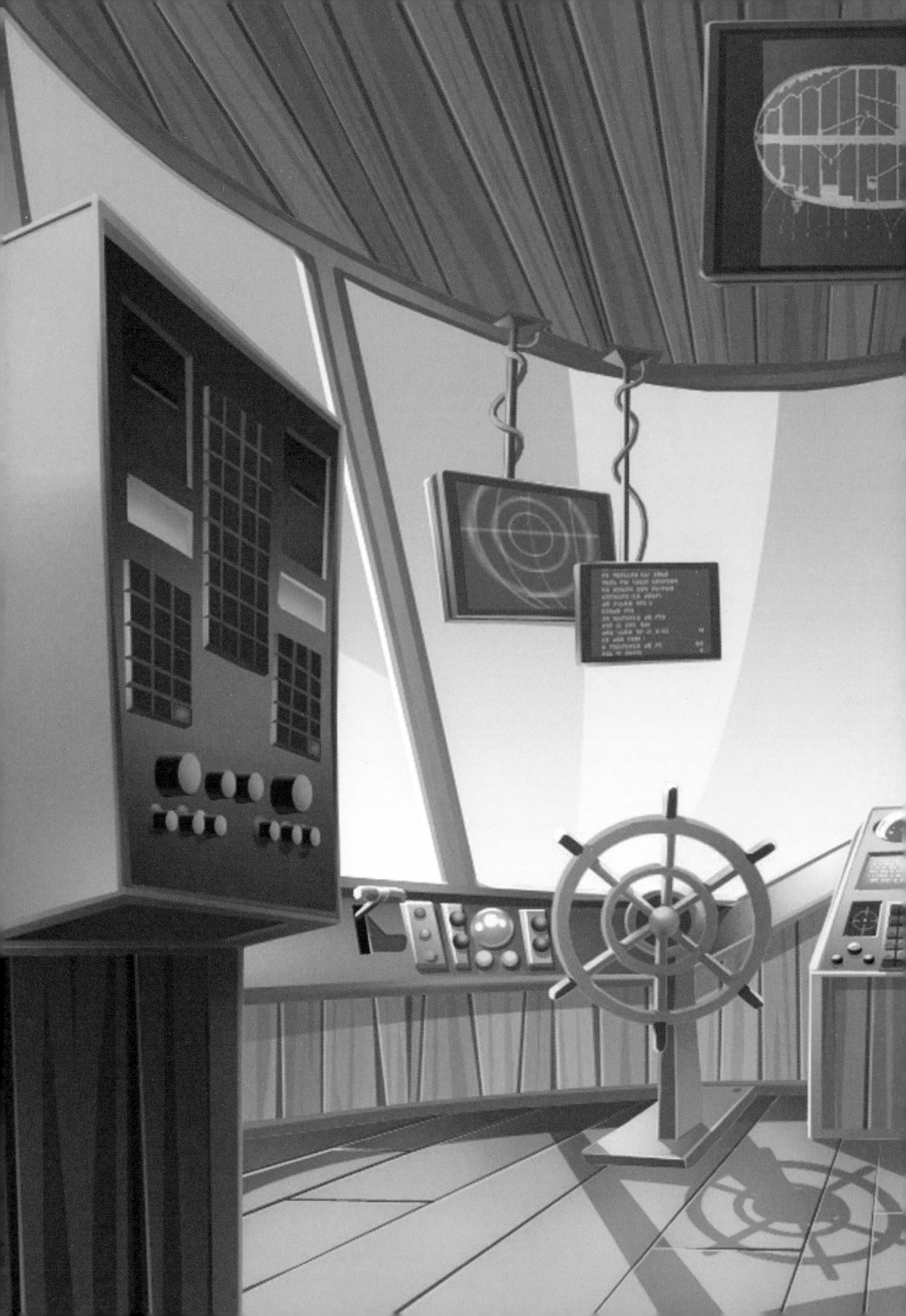